LOVE ME NOT

LOVE ME NOT

AYLA COX

Love Me Not

Copyright © 2025 Ayla Cox

Cover art: GetCovers

All rights reserved.

No part of this book may be reproduced or used in any form without the expressed and written permission of the copyright owner, except for the use of brief quotations for the purpose of book reviews and shit-talking.

This is a work of fiction. Any similarity between characters and situations to people, living or dead, is unintentional and purely coincidental. If such similarities to your life do exist within these pages, can you ask the sexy, tatted motorcycle man to be my bestie too?!

If you've happened upon a pirated copy of this novel, please remember that this author is independent and has spent thousands of hours creating this work of art. They deserve compensation for their art.

To reach Ayla, feel free to email her at:

AylaCoxWrites@gmail.com.

Contents

DEDICATION	4
PROLOGUE	6
CHAPTER 1	14
CHAPTER 2	26
CHAPTER 3	36
CHAPTER 4	50
CHAPTER 5	64
CHAPTER 6	76
CHAPTER 7	88
CHAPTER 8	104
CHAPTER 9	118
CHAPTER 10	132
CHAPTER 11	142
CHAPTER 12	156
CHAPTER 13	172
CHAPTER 14	180

CHAPTER 15	**188**
CHAPTER 16	**198**
EPILOGUE	**204**
FROM AYLA'S DESK	**218**
ABOUT AYLA	**220**
MORE FROM AYLA	**222**

Dedication

To everyone who has ever been done wrong:
You could've set their house on fire and you refrained.
I see you.

Prologue

Three years ago

Nothing killed a vibe faster than a pissed-off bitch in a skin-tight black jumpsuit with fire-red lipstick, and stilettos sharp enough to pierce someone's soul. Spoiler alert: I was the bitch, and I was there to set fire to the whole entire charade.

"Oh look, a cheating, spineless limp dick—"

The flash of paparazzi cameras danced across Fiona Lane's perfectly contoured cheekbones as her plastic smile faltered. Oh, she finally saw me. Good. Her gaze flitted to the side, scanning around her for security—or maybe an exit—but it was too late for that, babycakes. Far. Too. Late.

"Cass! What are you doing here?" Fiona interrupted, her voice brittle under that saccharine Hollywood charade. Her eyes were wide, almost pleading, but I didn't give a fuck.

It was her big night. This was her first major film premiere, but instead of basking in the glow of public adoration and smiling for the cameras, she was staring down the barrel of the person she'd screwed over.

Me.

I gave her a toothy, smile as I raised my voice, ensuring every single photographer, gossip columnist, and human with ear holes in the vicinity heard me loud and clear.

"I'm here to support the arts! Isn't that what you were doing when you were bouncing on my boyfriend's mediocre dick between takes? Acting?"

Gasps rippled through the crowd. Whoever wasn't paying attention to me was looking at me now. Cameras pivoted as murmurs grew louder. Fiona's ivory gown fluttered as she stepped back, her face quickly lost its color beneath the lights.

That's when the man who, from now on, would only be referred to as Shrek—my ex-boyfriend—stumbled over. He was towering, awkward, and looking more ogre-like than ever under the glare of a thousand camera flashes. His hand half-lifted as if to calm me down, to contain the explosion that was already mid-detonation.

"Don't you even try," I snapped, putting my finger in his face. "I was done talking to you a month ago. But since you insist..."

I spun toward the crowd, spreading my arms wide. "Was this bitch really pegging you while you called her Daddy? That's a little crazy, Shrek."

The scandalized, collective gasp swept the red carpet, and I turned back to see shame and anger on his face. Ahh, sweet, sweet payback.

Fiona stumbled back on her heels, spinning wildly as she looked around for help. "Security!" she shrieked. "Security! Get this fat bitch off my carpet!"

There she was—the real Fiona. Not the polished starlet or the influencer sweetheart, but the cruel jerk that had made my life a chaotic mess for years before she'd helped herself to my idiot boyfriend.

Honestly, her words didn't even sting. Nothing she said or did would be worse than finding out that the people closest to me had been deceiving me for months.

Shrek's jaw was practically detached and dragging on the ground. His pale skin was ghost white and he looked ready to faint. It was almost poetic—him looking like a possum faking dead and me standing there drenched in a righteous rage that lit a fire under the balls of my feet.

This was probably the time to run, to leave them in the messy wreckage of their truths—but I wasn't done. I swiped two champagne flutes from a passing tray, raising them high.

"A toast," I shouted, "To the horrible humans—" Four people were running at me. I needed to wrap this up. "Fuck it." I threw both flutes, straight into their faces.

Fiona let out a sound somewhere between a squeal and a gargle as champagne soaked her gown and dripped from her perfectly coiffed hair. Shrek just stood there, blinking slowly like his brain was buffering.

It was superb.

Security lunged for me, but I was already moving. I tossed the glasses and toed off the torture devices on my feet before vaulting the velvet security fence with a grace my big ass had never and would never possess again. My bare feet hit the cold pavement and I wobbled, but I didn't fall. In celebration, I snatched another glass of champagne from a passing caterer because why not?

I jogged away from the chatter of security guards crackling over radios and paparazzi cameras clicking. Fiona continued to screech and melt down, and it was precisely the symphony of chaos I'd wanted. Now, I just needed to find a getaway. I hadn't thought that far ahead. The cameras were following me.

Shit.

For a split second, time froze. The bright lights, clicking cameras, and questions directed at me, the sharp edge of Fiona's voice—it all blurred into noisy static. And, through the chaos, I spotted him.

Malik.

Leaning casually against a matte-black motorcycle, he watched me with that infuriating, knowing expression.

Of course, he was here and watching.

Malik and I had met years ago. He was the oil to my water, but we had built a friendship that jumped from texting to me spending time in his tattoo parlor. An hour ago, I'd sent him a message about my plan, and he'd tried to talk me out of it. But there he was: a knight in jeans and a hoodie.

"Barefoot in Hollywood?" he drawled in that southern good boy accent while raising one of his bushy eyebrows.

"You couldn't let me just do it on my own." I gave him a small frown before it morphed into a smile, "But did that look as good as it felt?" I asked, sipping the champagne with my pinky out like I was having tea with Queen Elizabeth.

"Better," he said. He paused, looking me up and down. "How'd you manage to jump the barrier in that outfit?"

"Talent."

He huffed out a laugh and swung one leg over the motorcycle. The engine growled to life beneath him, low and menacing. He pulled a helmet off the back of the bike and handed it to me.

"Ready for your getaway ride, or do you want to set the building on fire first?" he asked, putting his own helmet back on.

I glanced back at the premiere chaos and briefly considered it. The nerve to be parading around two weeks before Valentine's Day after ruining my fucking life. Taking a beat, I closed my eyes and breathed in the smell of him. Leather, a little gasoline, and a musky cologne that I absolutely needed the name of.

Yeah, I was done.

I tossed the empty champagne glass and the heels into a nearby trash can as I shoved the helmet over my braids before swinging onto the back of the motorcycle. It was wide and surging beneath me. I leaned forward and grabbed him tight around the waist.

"Oof," he fake wheezed.

"You've been trying to get me on this monstrosity for years. Let's go, already," I yelled over the sounds of him revving the engine. The paparazzi were standing off to the side, shouting questions as he peeled away from the street.

As we sped through Hollywood, wind whipping past me and the city lights blurring, something tight and heavy inside my chest loosened. I felt better. I wasn't carrying the weight of all this pain alone now. Maybe I was rash and that was too much.

But if love is war, then I was happy to be the motherfucking mushroom cloud.

Chapter 1

Did I regret going viral for calling out an ain't shit man and a knock-off Barbie doll in front of the entire world? Nope. Did I regret throwing a Molotov cocktail right at my young and burgeoning career with style and pizzazz? Occasionally. Sometimes. Mostly on the days I paid my bills.

That night wasn't just a moment of delicious, juicy revenge—it was an explosion. And the fallout? Well, I was still picking up the pieces three years later.

Sure, I'd been struggling to find steady work since I went nuclear on a romcom red carpet, but there were some things that I could rely on. Like having a friend who decorated my skin for cheap. Okay, he gave me the tattoos for free, but I did stuff for him and the other artists here, too!

It was January, my second least favorite month, and I was in Malik's chair, zoning out as the hum of the tattoo gun filled my ears, and he worked his magic on my skin. The sharp sting of the needle was grounding, almost meditative. His focus was absolute, his brow furrowed as he worked on the intricate floral design blooming across my bicep.

He was the only person I trusted to turn my body into a canvas. And his work was absolutely incredible. That's why he got paid the big bucks... just not by me.

MalInked had become my second home. I spent more time here than I did in my own apartment. I'd come and help out between gigs doing all the shit he hated like balancing the books and applying for permits. Hell, since the personal assistant work was slow, I started helping with inventory too.

What they don't tell you about your face getting plastered all over news articles and exposés is that they're cyclical. Memes, reaction videos, and songs came back every year like clockwork making it so that my infamy never died.

And I hated that for me.

"You're quiet today," he said, his voice low, warm, and a little scratchy—like caramel drizzled over concrete. "Thinking about your next stunt?

I laughed, turning to meet his eyes. "Nah. I've hung up my drama queen tiara. I'm retired. Reformed. I'm basically a nun now."

He let out a low chuckle, shaking his head slightly as he wiped excess ink from my arm. "Right. And I'm a virgin."

I snorted. "The man who I caught hiding butt naked in the bushes because some girl locked him out is suddenly celibate. Adorable."

He rolled his eyes, but his smile was genuine as he refocused on the tattoo. The weight of his hand on my arm was steady and comforting. He had this way of making everything feel... still. Like the noise of the world quieted down when he was around.

We'd grown close after the red carpet fiasco. Honestly, he was the only person that I felt that I could trust. He'd seen me at my worst. Arguably, I still was at my worst, but he didn't hold it against me.

Thankfully, it was just us in the shop tonight. Getting recognized made me want to crawl in a hole and perish.

"You still throwing your *Love Me Not* party this year?" Malik asked, his voice cutting through the buzz of the tattoo machine.

My stomach pitched and I had to fight to keep the disdain off my face. I'd thrown the first *Love Me Not* party a few weeks after the meltdown. I thought they'd find a new story but when February came around my face was still everywhere. Every magazine, every gossip blog, every social media account dissecting my viral humiliation.

So, I did what any sane human would—I threw a party. After calling in a favor I booked a room and threw the first *Love Me Not*: an aggressive and loud anti-Valentine's Day party where Hollywood could drink overpriced cocktails, play games, and laugh at the con that is romance. And it worked. People were so distracted by the party that the memes and the videos pivoted to talking about my audacity to give love the finger.

It worked for a little while, and then the anniversary came up and so did the memes. So, I made it an annual thing. We sold a lot of tickets, but the jobs I'd been hoping to get hired for hadn't come. Sure, a few folks were hiring me again for small things, but nothing big. Nothing that would put me back where I'd been when I was working for Fiona.

And I understood. I was a liability. They didn't need to know the whole story about what happened, all they knew was I could spectacularly lose my shit in front of everyone and spill secrets.

Yeah, I'd won in the court of public opinion. But in Hollywood? Not so much.

My expectation was that I'd be further along by now. I thought that I would be getting more jobs and finding my way. But I was still stuck in this weird limbo. How the hell was I supposed to pull off a party when I felt like I was still piecing my life back together?

But I couldn't tell him that. I never let him see that part of me. I never let anyone see the cracks. Not anymore.

"Of course," I said, forcing my voice to stay light. "Nothing says, 'I'm totally fine,' like hosting an annual anti-love gala for the C-listers and influencers with too much money and not enough therapy."

Malik didn't respond right away, his focus fixed on the shading of some small petals. When he finally spoke, his voice was softer. "You ever think about...letting this whole thing go? Releasing all the rage and moving on?"

The question hit me right in the chest. I looked away, focusing on the half-empty bottle of green soap on his tray.

"Moving on to what, exactly?" I let out a bitter laugh, but it came out weaker than I intended. "I'm not a cheesy movie." My voice wobbled slightly, and I could feel his eyes on me—watching. I kept talking to distract myself from the way he was looking right through me. "Half the people who hire me beg me to tell them all the juicy details of my heartbreak. This is my life now. It's fine."

He sighed softly, setting down the tattoo gun. The relaxing buzz faded, leaving a strange quiet in its place. His gloved fingers wiped up and down my upper arm with gentle, practiced care before wrapping it in plastic.

"You let it go, not because you have to, but because you deserve to. You gotta move forward." His attention was on securing the covering, so he didn't see the way my breath caught, and my eyes widened. Then he continued to gut punch me. "You're good at pretending you're good with it, but I know better," he said, his voice steady but edged with something heavy.

I flinched—barely—but he caught it. Looking away, I patted my arm, glad the numbing spray hadn't worn off just yet. Yes, I used the numbing spray. Argue with Jesus and your momma, not me.

Sitting up, I shrugged back on my leather jacket like it was armor and changed the subject. "You coming to the party or not?"

His brown eyes stayed locked on mine, searching. He was always doing that—looking at me like he might be able to see past the walls, past the sassy bitch, past the armor. Whatever he was looking for, he wasn't going to find it. I wasn't that Cassia anymore. This Cassia was a locked-down vault.

"Yeah, Cass. I'll be there," he said, rolling everything up and stuffing it into the trash.

I hopped off the chair, tugging at the hem of my jacket as if that would somehow settle the knot in my stomach that appeared whenever I thought about this stupid fucking party.

"Don't be late," I said, forcing a grin onto my lips.

Malik leaned back against his station, arms crossing over his broad chest. The mosaic of dark ink on his sleeves caught the light. The intricate tattoos were bold against his chestnut skin. But my second-favorite, the honeycomb circling his throat, bobbed as he looked me up and down.

"Wouldn't miss it for the world," he said low.

The chilly February air hit me like a slap as I stepped out of *MalInked* and onto the cracked pavement. I looked up at the inky sky, sad that light pollution robbed me of my favorite thing to look at: the stars. Dodging what looked like and probably was a human-sized shit, I shoved my hands deep into my pockets as I started walking. Hollywood wasn't for the meek. After nearly a decade, I was used to all manner of weird shit.

Turning on to Sunset Boulevard, the Valentine's Day decorations were everywhere—pink hearts taped to storefronts, glitter banners hanging between lampposts, and teddy bears so obnoxiously large they'd probably count as an extra person for the carpool lane.

The sidewalks were crowded with couples holding hands, window shopping, and sharing quiet smiles. The cute and obnoxious love of love was nauseating. I frowned as I took it all in. Had they not been bruised and beaten down by the universe too? Or was that just my shit luck?

Fuck, I hated this time of year.

For all the noise, the chatter, and the movement, everything felt... hollow. Like I was watching it all through foggy glass. I ducked into the iron bar-clad liquor store right around the corner from my house. The bell above the door jingled as I stepped inside.

The place was bright and quiet, the shelves stacked with colorful snacks and drinks. There was a man behind the counter I didn't recognize. He had tired eyes and a beanie pulled halfway over his forehead When I walked by, he glanced at me and recognition lit his face.

"Valentine's blues?" he asked, smirking faintly.

I grabbed a pack of gum and a candy bar, dropping them onto the counter. "Something like that," I replied.

He scanned my items, his leer softening into something closer to sympathy. I tapped my card and grabbed the bag.

"Hang in there, Renegade," he said as I turned to leave.

I didn't respond as I stepped back out into the cold. A day would go by without me being recognized, eventually. Obviously, it wasn't today. But there was always tomorrow.

Five minutes later, I finally made it to my apartment, I realized I'd taken the long way home without even meaning to. My apartment sat in an older building, close enough to Santa Monica Boulevard that I could hear the occasional siren wail or the distant bass from a club. The rent was atrocious, but I was making it work.

I unlocked the door, the familiar creak of the hinges the only thing that greeted me. The apartment was small but cozy—an exposed brick wall on one side, mismatched furniture on the other. My couch was draped in a fuzzy throw blanket, and a half-empty bottle of wine sat on the coffee table beside my laptop.

I tossed my keys onto the counter and flopped onto the couch, the springs groaning beneath me. The quiet was suffocating. I stared at the ceiling, my eyes following the cracks in the plaster and turning them into constellations. Tonight, I saw Pegasus mid-flight. My phone buzzed on the armrest beside me, but I ignored it.

My mind drifted back to Malik's question.

"You ever think about letting it all go, Cass? Moving on?"

Letting go sounded good—clean and final. But, letting go would mean admitting that some part of me had been holding on. Holding on to the betrayal, anger, and humiliation that still clung to me like a layer of sticky sweat on a hot day. Nope. I didn't want to think about it anymore.

Sitting up, I grabbed the wine bottle and found my way to the kitchen for a glass. I poured the last dregs into a somewhat clean mug. It wasn't classy, but neither was I. Not anymore. I looked in the cabinet before I remembered that the empty bottle in my hand was my emergency bottle.

Damn it all to hell. I grumbled my way back to the couch with my coffee cup. There went my evening plans of getting and staying drunk. And of course, the numbing was starting to wear off and I could feel the throbbing pain in my arm.

I threw my body on to the couch, taking a sip from the mug and resisting the urge to massage my arm. My phone buzzed again. This time, I glanced at the screen. It was an email from someone I didn't recognize. Putting the phone down, I took another sip before curiosity won out, and I opened my laptop and navigated to my emails.

Subject:

Opportunity: Once Upon a Crashout? Feature.

I froze with the mug halfway to my lips. The words stared back at me, black and bold against the white background. Something in my stomach twisted hard enough to make me feel nauseous. I sat the mug down and pressed my fingers against my temples.

I'd seen dozens of clips from the show. They tracked down people from viral moments and gave them the opportunity to speak about their experiences and what life became after their brush with fame. The last person featured on it got a podcast deal. My heart was in my throat.

The email was waiting for me to open it. It was a chance to stage a grand comeback, to tell my side of what happened and explain why I'd done what I did. But instead of feeling excited, all I felt was apprehensive. The cursor turned into a little hand, it was ready for me to click.

I couldn't do it.

I closed the laptop. Tomorrow. I'd deal with it tomorrow. For now, I was leaning back on the couch, staring at the cracked ceiling, and letting myself pretend—for just a few minutes—that the cracks were Andromeda and everything around me wasn't a crumbled mess.

Chapter 2

It had been four hours since I slammed my laptop shut. Four hours of pacing and a brief five-minute interlude where I screamed into a pillow.

I still hadn't opened the email. And I was practically crawling out of my skin. Instead of doing anything productive—like, ya know, facing my problems—my thumbs found their way to my text thread with Malik.

You still at the shop?

His reply took a few minutes.

Yeah. What's up?

I shrugged on my jacket and pulled on my sneakers.

On my way. Don't leave.

He didn't reply after that, but he didn't need to. Malik was Malik—dependable as hell. He'd be there, probably knee-deep in some paperwork, patiently waiting for me to bring whatever I was stewing in.

And this one? It was a doozy-doo as my grammy used to say.

Twenty minutes later, I stood outside *MalInked*. The shop windows were tinted a chromatic silver. It was meant to keep the client's private. Fluorescent lights glowed, showing off *MalInked*'s logo, a wave in the shape of a hand drawing, lighting up the uneven sidewalk.

I pushed the door open, the heat of the shop surrounding me as I stepped inside to the smell of antiseptic, cleaning supplies, and faint traces of cologne. The scent was familiar and wrapped around me like a weirdly comforting hug.

The man himself was hunched over his chair, his tattoo gun buzzing softly. I was a little surprised he had a client this late, but having your own shop meant you could work your own hours. If he'd told me he had a client, I'd have just spiraled at home. I flipped the lock as both of their heads turned toward me.

A brown-skinned woman was sprawled across his chair, looking like she'd stepped off the set of an edgy Bollywood drama. Electric-blue pixie cut, combat boots dangling off the chair, and a Louis Vuitton hoodie had the sleeves pulled all the way up. She pulled out her headphones as Malik gave me a disapproving frown.

"You didn't walk here, did you?" he asked.

I rolled my eyes, blowing off his grumpy *this area isn't safe* tone. "Don't frown, people will think you're the surly one."

The woman cocked her head. "Wait a second... You're Cassia James."

Dropping into the worn leather chair across from them, I asked, "Are you about to ask me to autograph your tits?"

She barked out a laugh, loud and unfiltered. "Oh, I like her." She smacked his arm. "Why didn't you tell me you knew the Renegade herself?"

"Because I was busy minding my business, Jade," he said, dryly.

Jade waved him off with a wave of her tattooed fingers. "Yeah, yeah. Whatever."

"Jade, huh? Nice to meet you. I'm Cass, walking PR disaster and retired chaos goblin. At your service."

"Pleasure, babe," Jade said, giving me a mock salute. "So, are we about to witness some *real* drama, or did you just miss Malik's dumb puppy-dog face?"

His brows furrowed. "Puppy-dog?"

"You know," Jade said, "The cute, *I'm so hungry, hug me, play with me, love me* look."

I cackled. "Oh my god, he does have that face. That's a good poochie."

We laughed as he sighed, muttering something under his breath about "better clients" before refocusing on Jade's tattoo.

"Didn't you come here for a reason?" he asked. I gave him a look before he shifted his eyes to Jade and nodded. He was an excellent judge of character. If he said Jade was cool, she was cool.

Sighing, I leaned back, gently pulling my phone from my pocket and holding it out with two fingers like it might explode in my hand. Malik was back to sketching a line as Jade watched me, curious and waiting.

I was glad it was after hours because if the whole shop was full, I'd have aborted the mission and taken my ass home. He cleared his throat and started pulling at Jade's skin and moving the needle across her wrist while she leaned forward, looking me dead in the face.

"Out with it. You're more dramatic than my Naani!"

"Fine, fine." I pressed my palm against my thigh, grounding myself. "I got an email. But I haven't read it yet."

Two pairs of eyes pinned me in place. Neither of them said a word, but I read their intent clear as day.

"Okay, I'll just read it." I cleared my throat, suddenly feeling vulnerable under both their gazes, and shifted a bit before I clicked on the email.

> **Dear Ms. James,**
>
> **We reached out and left a voicemail, but we also thought this message might find you here. I'm contacting you on behalf of *Once Upon a Crashout*. We saw that you'd sent out invitations for this year's Love Me Not party, and we'd love to feature you and our new #Reclaimed segment.**
>
> **Since the party is next week, we'd need to move fast. This would be a chance for you to share your story in your own words and explain what happened on that Valentine's Day in 2022. We're thinking we'll release**

the segment and then live stream your party! We'd love to talk numbers with you if you're interested.

Thanks so much for hearing us out,

Travis, Exec Producer at Once Films

The buzz of the tattoo machine stopped as Malik turned to me. His stool creaked as he analyzed my face, trying to decipher how I felt about the whole thing. Maybe he could tell me because I was confused as all hell. A part of me was hopeful, but the jaded bitch inside was suspicious of the entire thing.

"An engraved invitation to let the internet rip me apart again. How thoughtful," I said, dropping the phone onto my lap.

He set the tattoo gun down and gave me one of his sweet Malik looks—steady, warm, and stubborn in that way only he could pull off. "You're worried over an email? Cass, you could handle this blindfolded."

I gave him the Cassia look—incredulous, annoyed, and spicy.

"You've been hiding for years." He spoke over me as I tried to interject, "You throw these parties, disappear halfway through, and then go silent on social media for another year. This is your chance, Cass. To own the chaos instead of letting it own you."

"Or," Jade piped up, twirling her phone charger like a lasso. "You can just... fake it?"

Malik and I turned to her in unison.

"Fake it?" I asked slowly.

She nodded, her grin sharp and conspiratorial. "Babe, this is LA. That's the game. Throw the *Love Me Not* party, smile for the cameras, and parade this tattooed Hunk-ules around like he's your hot, mysterious boyfriend. Boom."

Malik froze mid-wipe, his tattoo needle hovering above Jade's arm. His brows furrowed, and he blinked. "First, I was a dog, and now I'm Hunk-ules?"

"Shh. I'm getting to her," Jade said, waving a hand in his face and leaning toward me. "Tell me that's not PR gold?"

I gaped at both of them. "This is either a genius plan or the opening scene of a true-crime podcast."

Jade shrugged. "Maybe. But is it *wrong*?"

He tilted his head, his soft smile creeping back. "She's not off-base, Cass. I can be your Hunk-ules."

"Oh my god," I groaned, dragging my hands down my face. "You two are in cahoots. This is like that Sandra Bullock movie."

"*While You Were Sleeping?*" Jade asked.

"*Speed?*" Malik offered.

"*Speed*? No! *The Proposal*." I said, feeling even more annoyed.

"So, you want to pretend to be engaged too?" He grinned so hard I could practically see his tonsils.

"What? No. Ugh. Forget I said it," I grumbled.

Jade laughed. "Babe. Smoke. And. Mirrors. Sell the illusion and the rest will follow."

I sighed, the weight of the conversation settling over my foggy brain like a thick, hot blanket.

"Fine. Fine! I'll *think* about it."

"The proposal?" Malik asked, laughing.

"The fake boyfriend. Don't piss me off, Malik," I said, scowling.

Jade clapped her hands together. "That's the spirit!" Her grin widened. "I also take bribes. VIP bribes. I wanna be close enough to smell the champagne and regret."

I stepped back, laughing at her. "Alright, Smurfette. VIP access it is." I held out my pinky, and she locked it with her own.

The tattoo gun started to buzz again as he grabbed her hand and brought the needle back to her skin.

"Good. Now, I've got another hour on this, and then I'll take you home," he said without looking up.

I groaned, but then he gave me the other Malik look—serious as hell, bossy, and kinda hot. Since I was stuck here for a little longer, I sat back down and kicked my feet up, turning to Jade.

"Did you know that Malik used to have a soul patch?" I asked.

"He what?" Jade screeched.

"I regret every decision that has led me to this moment," he said.

As I sat there, watching him work his magic along Jade's wrist, I realized that for the first time in years, I was feeling hopeful. If anyone could help me do this, it was Malik.

Chapter 3

Malik didn't, in fact, need an hour, but two. We'd spent that time talking about movies with Jade. Her dad had produced a few really good ones, and she regaled us with some stories, one of which involved an A-lister, a can of whipped cream, and a block of cheese. Celebrities are weird, man.

It was almost noon when I finally rolled out of bed and wandered into the kitchen to start my day. I threw a cup of water into the microwave and half-wheezed, half-cried as I spooned in some instant coffee and stirred.

Closing my eyes, I dreamed of lightly sweet espresso as I sipped.

My eyes drifted to my computer thrown haphazardly onto the couch cushion, and I wondered how much espresso I could buy with the money they were going to offer me. The trick was, I'd need to reply to the email to find out.

Taking my lackluster cup of coffee, I flopped onto the couch and opened my laptop.

The email subject line glared at me: **"Opportunity: Where Are They Now? Feature"**

I placed my coffee down and cracked my knuckles like I was about to hack into the Pentagon's servers.

"Okay, Cass. You can do this," I said, psyching myself up. "Open the email. Pretend to be a functional adult."

My fingers hovered over the keys as I typed:

"Dear Travis..."

Ugh. No. Delete.

"Hi Travis, thanks for reaching out—"

Absolutely not. Delete.

"Okay, fine, Travis, let's do this thing—"

Delete. Delete. Delete.

I groaned, flopping backward dramatically and staring at the ceiling like it had all the answers. After a minute, I sat up, gritted my teeth, and typed out something that didn't sound completely insane. I hoped.

Send.

The swish effect echoed around the room and my heart dropped into my ass.

"Oh fuck. I did it," I wheezed before slamming the laptop shut and staring at it like it was going to self-destruct in ten seconds.

Without hesitation, I picked up my phone and dialed Malik. He'd answer because he knew I hated talking on the phone as much as I hated green beans and that little dangly thing that swings in the back of my throat.

"Hey, you okay?" his voice was scratchy. He'd probably just woken up and was absolutely not ready for the mess of chaotic energy I was getting ready to throw at him.

"No, Malik, I am *not* okay. I've just signed up to be a spectacle, all so I can feed myself and live. I didn't ask to be here. Who wants to be born just to pay bills and die?"

He chuckled, and I could hear his sweet, wide smile through the phone. "Cass, this isn't a horror movie. It's an opportunity. And you've got me as your emotional support sidekick."

My chest got all warm. I knew he'd said it last night. But late nights made both of us a little loopy. I don't know why him saying the words again helped, but they did. Knowing I had someone in my corner, even when I was the grumpiest bitch on the planet, made me feel better.

"You're serious?" I asked, my voice quiet.

"Yeah. I am," he said. His voice was so steady, so sure. I could feel the chaos in my brain dying down just because it could hear his voice and feel his calm energy flowing through me.

"Okay. Okay," I said, sucking in a sharp breath. "Are you busy? I need... I don't know. A plan? A fast-forward button?"

"I'm on my way. And I'm bringing snacks."

The line went dead, and I sank onto the couch, phone clutched to my chest. There was literally no one else I trusted to be there for me the way Malik was—the way he had been for years. Every time I felt like the world was gathering to fall on top of me, he appeared with his save-a-Cass cape on, a smile on his face, and a joke or compliment to pull me out of my doom spiral.

If it wasn't for him, I'd have left Hollywood right after the-event-that-shall-not-be-named. He's the only reason I was still there, still standing. Losing my closest friend and the man I'd been dating for years was one of the hardest things I'd ever had to experience. And Malik was a rock through it all. I'd always appreciated him for that.

While I was waiting, I caught up with a few of the vendors for the party, ensuring that they'd all gotten their portion of the ticket sales. We'd sold a few tickets, but not as many as the year before or the year before that. The fun of the event was probably wearing off.

I usually got a few odd PA jobs out of it when my name hit the gossip headlines. Between those and the profit I made off the party, I'd get a little bit of breathing room financially for a few months. But after paying for vendors, security, food, and booze, I wasn't exactly swimming in enough profits to get me through. I needed work—steady work.

I was fielding email requests for influencers when Malik walked in forty-five minutes later. He was carrying two iced coffees, a bag of sour gummy rings, and a greasy bag from the taco truck down the street.

"A true hero," I said, grabbing the cup of sludge I'd made for myself and pushing it over to the side. He dropped everything onto the table, and I hugged him around the center, tightening my hold on his waist and shoving my face into his chest.

"Alright, alright," he whispered above me. "Your carnitas are getting cold."

"You even bought me carnitas?" I squealed, letting him go so I could dive for the bag.

"I don't dig on swine, but I know you like it," he said as I tore open the bag and took a hearty sip of the coffee, he'd brought me.

"You are a marvel. A light in the darkness. The wind beneath my wings," I sang off-key.

"Yeah, yeah," he replied, folding himself up on my couch and grabbing the chicken tacos he'd bought for himself.

"So, what are you thinking?" he asked, taco juice was dribbling down his chin. I grabbed a napkin and wiped his face.

"Well, we need off-limits topics, right?" I asked.

He nodded and I pulled out a notepad and wrote that down to think about later.

Chewing on a slice of red onion, he asked, "And the party?"

"That's the fun part. I show up, look amazing, and sell the illusion. And then you'll be my fake boyfriend," I said, mid-chew, oil dripping down my arm.

"I'm thinking of giving the role more gravitas. Broody, mysterious boyfriend." He threw up a hand to illustrate his point and gave me a flat look that lasted all of five seconds before he started to laugh.

I snorted. "Broody? You're about as broody as a bucket of sunshine."

"I can be broody!" he protested.

I gave him a look.

He sighed. "Fine. I'll just... stand there and look mysterious."

"Better."

Despite the mood, something heavy settled in my chest. I looked down at my list and frowned, tapping my pen against the paper.

"What am I doing?"

I was doing all this work to get back to where I was before, but did I really like the path that I was on? When I'd met Malik, I was a burnt out mess. Fiona had me running in so many directions at once, but I didn't mind because we were friends. But what if it wasn't Fiona, what if it was the job itself?

"I don't think that's the question, Cass. Do you remember when I was stressed out, having spent all that time traveling? You asked me something. And now I'm asking you: what is it that you want?" he asked, sipping at his americano.

Giving myself a moment, I sat back. What *did* I want? Mostly, I needed to provide context. The story had gotten so out of hand, Shrek and Fiona were making all of this bullshit up, and I'd just let them. People needed to hear from me.

"To tell the truth. But what if it backfires on me?" I asked quietly.

"It won't," he said simply. "And we're not going to entertain the what-ifs."

And, crazy as it was, I believed him.

I finished up my tacos as he checked his phone. I was wrapping up the trash as his eyes flickered down to the Scrabble board tucked under my coffee table, and I tried to ignore him.

"You know what you need, Cass?" he asked. He was using that tone he'd get when he wanted to bamboozle me, but I wasn't going to fold.

"Therapy? An exorcism?" I offered, waving my hands dramatically as I retreated to the trash can, hoping I'd distracted him.

"Well, yes. But also—Scrabble."

I groaned, "No. Absolutely not. You're a menace every time."

But he was already pulling out the board, setting it between us with practiced ease.

"Malik," I groaned.

"Come on. It'll cheer you up," he said, fondling the bag like a ball sack.

I knew that it wasn't going to end well. I hated losing and whenever we played, he'd crush me. But I flopped down and readied myself for battle.

As expected, the game was pure chaos.

He was playing the wildest words I'd ever seen on the game board, like *QUIXOTIC* and *JOUSTED*. Where I was barely making points with *BRAINY* and *LADYLIKE*.

I was trailing by two hundred points as I beat my head against the couch cushion. He placed his tiles down and played off my newest word, calling out his points.

"Vrow? Are you summoning ancient spirits? Is this a séance?" I wailed, looking at the chalkboard that had our scores.

"I don't know, but I know it's a valid word," he said with his cheeky smile.

My fingers flew over my phone screen, and I saw that it was, in fact, a valid word. I picked up a pillow and wondered if I could suffocate myself. "This isn't fun!" I whined. "You're supposed to let me win!"

"When did I say that?" he laughed.

I slid to the floor.

"No mercy," he said, grinning. "Losing builds character."

I flopped around on the carpet, arms spread wide for maximum effect. "This game sucks. Words suck. You suck."

He leaned over the board, beaming. "Admit it, you'd perish without me."

Scoffing, I covered my eyes, hoping for someone to appear and save me from my current misery.

"Your turn, Cassia," he called from above me.

I threw a tile at him.

The torturous game finally ended with him winning—obviously. He packed up the board while I stayed sprawled dramatically on the carpet. The floor was for losers, and it was my punishment.

Malik leaned down and lightly tapped at my sore arm under the baggy sweater I had on.

"No scratching, you'll ruin it." His tone was amused, but he was serious.

"I'll put something on it," I said, letting him help me to my feet.

"Hey."

I looked at him and he gave me a soft smile.

"You've got this, Cass. Now stop catastrophizing and go take a nap. I'll see you tomorrow?"

"Yeah," I said softly. "Tomorrow."

I watched him leave and looked at the email I'd seen twenty minutes ago.

Subject:

Scheduling a call—are you free in an hour?

My stomach flipped as I clicked it open and confirmed that that time worked for me, replying with my cell number.

Let's fucking go.

Chapter 4

The cursor on my document blinked at me. Was it mocking me? Did it have to flash at me and remind me that I was sitting here, procrastinating? I needed to prep, but I also couldn't believe it. I had just signed the contract. The *actual* contract. With my *actual* name.

It was official. Permanent. Carved in blood. Okay, I was being dramatic. But it was all set. The call with Travis had been smooth. Afterward, I'd rattled off my list of requirements to participate via email. I expected pushback, maybe even a finger emoji after being blocked, but, instead, he'd been thrilled to agree.

I'd been given final cut approval, a list of preapproved questions, an agreement to keep Malik's personal life off-limits, and an understanding that the live stream would only last an hour.

And the paycheck? Lord. The paycheck. I saw it and immediately went downstairs to buy myself a real coffee. It was everything I had hoped for and more.

And now I was staring at a Word document titled: *Pre-Interview Questions—Do Not Panic*.

Spoiler alert: I was absolutely fucking panicking. I scanned the list again, seeing the first and most important question resting at the top:

What do you want people to know about your side of the story?

I started typing.

> I'm not a supervillain. I mean, sure, I had my villain moment, but if you found out your bestie was stroking your boyfriend's poop chute, you'd lash out too. I'm a human being. But that one moment isn't who I am. Alright, I can

be like that sometimes. But not all the time!

My fingers hovered over the keyboard, and I moved to press the delete key as I reread my answer. But it was true. I was hurt. And I was betrayed. I had to be honest and raw—and messy— if this was going to work.

I moved on to the next question.

Do you regret how you handled the red carpet incident?

> Regret is a strong word. No. Yes? A little? I do regret that my personal bullshit affected my career. But calling them out? Not even a little. I trusted them both so much, and I couldn't just let them get away with what they did.

I groaned, throwing my arm over my face.

There had to be a reward for this. Alcohol. That could be my reward. And I had the perfect plan. It was Sunday and Malik's shop was closed. First step, I'd finish drafting these, and, second step, was tequila.

Definitely tequila.

When Malik opened his door, he had a toothbrush hanging out of his mouth and his sweatpants slung low on his hips. I tried and failed to divert my eyes from the taut muscles and lean man meat in my face. I'd seen him shirtless a few times, but it always gave me a weird feeling that I quickly stomped all over before setting it on fire.

Frowning, I pushed my way inside.

"It's past two and you're still rocking morning breath? You're really leaning into that tortured artist aesthetic, huh?"

He frowned before his eyebrows lifted at the two bottles of expensive tequila cradled in my arm like a newborn.

"You brought tequila," he said around the toothbrush, closing the door behind me.

"And tacos," I said, holding up the greasy brown paper bag. "Because I just did a big girl thing, and I deserve a drink."

He plucked one of the bottles from me, inspecting the label with a low whistle. "Cass, this is *ridiculous*. Did you rob a bank on your way here?"

I put down the second bottle and the tacos and headed for his kitchen for glasses and his stash of juice in the fridge.

"Signed a contract—sold my soul. Same diff," I said over my shoulder. "And cover up your titties, have you no decency?"

His warm, slightly chaotic apartment smelled like fresh laundry and something vaguely spicy—probably whatever he'd had for dinner.

His place had always been comfortable. Worn leather couch. A couple of mismatched throw pillows. Some signed posters from old movies were framed and hung haphazardly on the walls. It was very Malik.

"How you gonna come over here unannounced and judge how I walk around my house?" he yelled from the hallway as he wandered to his room.

"Oh, excuse me for surprising you with fancy shit. I was hoping we could get day drunk, but I can leave," I said, stomping my feet like I was leaving.

He turned the corner, tugging a shirt on as he looked me up and down. We both started laughing. Shaking his head, he moved backwards.

"Alright, I'm in," he said, dropping onto the couch and kicking up his bare feet onto the coffee table. "Ground rules. One: no crashing out. Two: no karaoke. Three: we finish at least one of these bottles."

"Deal...ish I can't guarantee that a song won't burst free," I replied, smiling at him, holding the juice in my hand like it was a prize. "Now, I just need the salt." My smile becoming a snigger.

'Cassia James, you put salt anywhere near this tequila, I'm sending your ass home," he growled playfully.

I cackled, grabbing the juice and glasses as I danced over to him.

An hour later, the tacos were gone, the tequila bottle was almost empty, and we were both practically one with the couch. Thankfully, Malik only lived a few blocks from me, I was going to be crawling home at this rate.

"So," he said, pointing at me, "what's your game plan for the party?"

"Look hot," I said, touching a finger.

He laughed, a low and warm sound from his chest. "Solid start."

"Sell the illusion," I said, wiggling my hand in front of his face as I raised a second finger.

"Seductive deceit" he drawled, giving me a look that lingered a little too much.

"Don't have a public meltdown," I said as I ticked off a third finger.

"Ah. That one's tricky."

I groaned, dropping my head onto his shoulder. "I know. I gotta woo-sah or something. I can't be all 'look at me, I'm well-adjusted' and then punch someone in the face."

"You'd never punch someone in the face," he said softly.

"I mean, I could," I grumbled.

"Sure," he said, giving me a look that said he absolutely didn't believe me.

He knew my grumpy bitch exterior was a front and I was really nice deep down. Deep, deep—deep down. After the whole debacle, I'd lost so many people who didn't want to be associated with my chaos, but he didn't leave.

I didn't know who I'd be if he hadn't breathed encouragement and positivity into me.

"And what's your plan?" I asked him, trying not to get misty-eyed at the thought.

"Pass out my card. Get new clients. Stay mysterious. Make sure you don't punch people," he rattled off, pouring himself a shot. I sighed, my tequila-soaked brain making everything feel a little softer around the edges.

He was going to be a great fake boyfriend.

Whoa, where'd that come from? It was the alcohol that was buzzing in my veins, syrupy and sweet. That's what had my insides all gooey. Yep. The booze. Suddenly, an idea slipped past my lips before I could stop it.

"You know..." I said slowly, "We should probably kiss." I drew out the words and looked over at him.

Malik froze before slowly turning to look at me like he was afraid I was going to attack him. "What now?"

"For practice!" I said quickly, sitting up and waving my hands as I got a teeny bit dizzy. "We can't just wing it. What if we're awkward in front of the cameras? What if—"

"Cass." His voice was soft and, and it instantly shut me up.

He leaned forward, just slightly, and my breath caught in my throat. The closer he came, the more his scent floated around me, cocooning me in woodsy citrus. It felt like it was all happening in slow motion. Had his lips always been so full? As his smooth fingers quested across my neck, he pulled my face forward. My stomach clenched as his relentless eye contact kept me prisoner.

My hand moved to his chest, feeling the heat of his skin through his shirt. I gasped.

His eyes flickered down to my lips, and I felt heat pooling low in my stomach. His thumb traced the edge of my lip, and I saw his pupils dilate as he leaned in...

His lips were *right there*. And for one fragile, heart-thundering moment, I wanted to close the distance and taste those lips. Run my lips along the seam. Feel his tongue tangling with mine.

I sputtered, pushing back away from him.

"Okay!" I blurted, too loud, too bright. "Yep. Experiment over. We're fine. We got this," I said as pleasure flowed heavily through my body, going right down to my throbbing lady bits.

The air felt heavy, thick with something I couldn't name. My heart was beating so hard in my ears that I was convinced it was going to break free from my chest and start flopping around on the ground before doing the electric slide. I could still feel the ghost of his thumb tracing my lip.

Nope. Absolutely not. Abort mission.

My core clenched as Malik sat back slowly, rubbing the back of his neck with a wry smile. "Yep. We got this," he said, his voice low. I could hear something buried in there that sounded like regret.

But it wasn't. Nope. We were friends. This was fake. And he was just doing his homegirl a solid.

We stared at each other for a long moment, and the air between us felt suffocating and hot. There was something different but familiar about the way he looked at me. And a small voice in the back of my mind wondered very loudly why I was afraid of what he would taste like. Why did I stop just shy of feeling his lips against mine? Why didn't I just reach forward and trace his skin with my tongue?

My eyes went on the same journey, bouncing from his lips to his exposed neck and his ear. Would his earlobes be sensitive if I ran my teeth along them? His gaze darkened as his eyes flitted down to my lips, and I took a stuttering breath as I stood and put distance between us.

Whatever the thing between us was—the spark, the heat—I had to escape it. I couldn't ruin the only friendship I had by randomly throwing myself at him. I'd never even looked at him like that. I wasn't going to now. My insides needed to chill.

It was the hunger strike. Yep. That's what it was. I hadn't had sex since Shrek had so thoroughly demolished my heart. But the only person who had even come close to waking me up was sitting on his couch, practically volunteering to be a lamb to the slaughter.

Or maybe he wasn't. And he was just doing what I'd asked, and I was being fucking weird about it. I had to leave. Fresh air. Water. Something.

"Okay, I'm gonna head home. The uh- the interview is in two days," I sputtered as I grabbed my bag and jacket.

"Let me know the time, I'll be there," he said, standing.

Jesus, the way his throat bobbed. I could just—

"You don't—"

His hand came to my chin, and I almost melted into a puddle on the floor.

"Let. Me. Know. The. Time." Each word ran through my body, and I swear to God I was so close to orgasm, I had to bite the inside of my cheek to keep from unraveling right there.

That charged silence was back, and I felt myself drifting towards him. He caught me around the waist as I swayed, and I looked up into his brown eyes. Watching the way his gaze got hooded as he looked down at me. There were little golden flecks near his pupil. How had I never noticed those before?

"You good?" he asked, his voice a full octave deeper than it normally was. I swear it vibrated all the way through me.

I needed to escape, but all I could think of was all the drunk thoughts that were threatening to spill from my lips. Filthy thoughts. Nasty thoughts. Thoughts involving sitting on his face and writhing my hips in circles until he begged me to let him breathe. Visions of holding him to me as he rocked inside me as he drove me crazy and made me scream his name.

"Umm." I pulled away from him and took a deep breath, only to find myself surrounded by the scent of him lingering around me. My gaze fell back to his lips, and I licked my own. He reached for me, and I had to leave before I did something really, really dumb.

"I'm okay. I'll text you," I said, stumbling away from him and out the door without looking back.

What the actual hell was going on? And how did I turn this all off? Because I couldn't want to fuck Malik. It was *Malik*. Ma. Lik. The man was a puppy dog. And I was a jerk. I couldn't want him. I liked my men emotionally unavailable and aloof.

And when did his face get all sexy?

My fingers ran along my lips the whole way home as I wondered—what if?

Chapter 5

The morning of the interview arrived far too quickly. I was ready but also, absolutely not ready. Not even a little bit. My palms were sweaty, my knees weak, and my arms were heavy. I got up way earlier than necessary and ran down to the local coffee shop to grab a drink.

The iced coffee in my hands was my security blanket as I tried to talk myself off the ledge. I'd spent the last two days trying not to think about almost kissing Malik, and it wasn't until that morning that I realized I was going to be on camera. I was scrolling through my document on my phone, reading and rereading the answers I'd written up for the questions.

"You're fine," I said, walking in circles in my living room. "It's just a conversation. You talk to people all the time. Except there's gonna be a camera. And lights. And at least a million people judging you while they take their morning shit."

Yeah, that wasn't helping. At all. My phone buzzed, and Malik's name popped up.

You awake?

The dots appeared as he continued typing before I replied.

Take a breath. Drink some water.

I snorted and rolled my eyes, before typing with my thumb.

And, no, coffee doesn't count as water. Nice try, smartass.

Letting out a loud laugh, I stopped typing and walked over to the kitchen. I put my coffee down and went to grab some water from the fridge.

I could practically hear the calm, firm tone of his voice. I could see the way he looked at me when I was being unreasonable. Drinking half the bottle, I put it on the counter and snapped a photo, texting it to him.

I'd spent an hour in the closet, finding the perfect nondescript outfit. Now I just needed to put on my sweater and head out the door. I cracked my neck and stepped into my flats. This was going to be fine.

I jotted out a text as I grabbed my purse.

Leaving now. If I get struck by lightning on the way, avenge me.

He sent a laughing emoji.

With my dying breath.

I shoved my phone into my bag, taking one last look at my outfit that I hoped screamed serious professional grown woman—the polar opposite of the catsuit I'd set fire to three years ago—and headed out the door.

Once Upon a Crashout did all their filming in a local studio on Gower, right by the iconic KTLA tower. I was able to drive there in under ten minutes, which surprised the hell out of me. Malik was standing in an empty spot in front of his motorcycle, and he waved me in. Parking behind his bike, I stepped out.

His arms were crossed over his chest. He'd embraced the whole tattooed biker heartthrob look, and he'd thankfully left his I-read-poetry cardigan at home. He was wearing all black—black jeans, black shirt, black boots—and I was certain he was doing it on purpose. The man had more color in his wardrobe than I did.

"Tall, dark, and mysterious," I said as I strolled up to him.

His head tilted, and his smile softened into something warmer as his gaze swept over me—pausing, briefly, at the neck of my cardigan. I swallowed, heat creeping up my neck. Why was he looking at me like that? Why did he have to smell so... so Malik?

Just the thought of the way his hand had felt against my skin made my stomach flop and flutter. My eyes locked in on the bobbing of his throat. The way that his tattoos danced as the skin moved had me tightening my thighs.

Seeing him in the flesh had me face to face with the uncomfortable truth I'd been ignoring. I'd blamed all that giddy bullshit on the tequila, but whatever flip I'd switched was still on. In the light of day. In the *sober* light of day.

Crap.

Had he always had that tiny little mole on his lip? Fuck. I was staring. I averted my eyes, making sure I absolutely didn't make eye contact. I'd fold like a lawn chair if he gave me any semblance of a look. Clearing my throat, I stepped around him.

"Let's get inside before I start sweating through my deodorant," I said.

He chuckled, falling into step beside me as we walked through the hallway and up the stairs. God, even his chuckle was making me feel things. First step, the interview. Second step, a vibrator and not thinking of Malik's face while I used it.

The studio was sleek and modern—LA minimalism at its finest. Malik dropped onto the couch with an ease I wish I was feeling. I felt my heart beating all the way in my ass, and I was still tossing back and forth which version of myself I wanted to show the world.

"Cassia."

I looked up, realizing that I'd been pacing for the last thirty seconds. He stood, closing the space between us in two smooth steps. His hands landed on my shoulders, firm but gentle, thumbs brushing my shoulders.

"Breathe."

I inhaled slowly. Exhaled shakily.

"Good." His voice was soft, steady, and so damn Malik it made my chest ache. "You've got this. You're gonna sit in that chair, look the camera dead in the lens, and remind the world exactly who you are. And if you start to panic, look at me. I'll be right there, I promise."

His words wrapped around me, warm and solid. How did he do that? How did he make everything feel so... still?

I nodded, swallowing hard. "You're freakishly good at this, you know that?"

He looked amused. "Because I know you, Cass. Better than most people do."

Before I could respond, someone popped out and smiled at me. "Ms. James? We're ready for you."

He gave my shoulders one last squeeze before stepping back. "Go knock 'em dead, Cass."

The assistant talked as we walked, "Any time you feel uncomfortable or want to start over, you let me know.

Thank you for adhering to all the guidelines we sent over, it really makes things go smoother." Her pace was brisk as she showed us to a studio in the back.

Showtime.

After a light dusting from the makeup artist, I was sitting down on the set. It was a dreamscape of soft lighting, strategically placed velvet chairs, and cameras positioned at angles that felt far too close to my face for comfort. The host, Nadia Lee, was perched across from my chair, glowing in a crimson blazer.

"Cassia, thank you so much for being here today," Nadia said with a practiced warmth that somehow still felt genuine.

"Thanks for having me," I replied, fighting to keep my voice from showing my nerves.

The first few questions were softballs—easy, breezy backstory chatter. How did I enjoy growing up in Missouri? Why Hollywood? My favorite projects. They weren't trying to spook me. Yet.

"So. Your relationship with Fiona and Chris," she said.

"Yes. I was dating Shrek while I worked for Fiona. Someone on set pulled me aside to tell me what they saw,

I couldn't believe it. Fiona thought it was fine. And I didn't."

Nadia's head tilted slightly, her voice dipping into a softer register. "What was going through your mind on that red carpet three years ago?"

My throat got tight. My palms became clammy. But then—right there, just behind the camera operator—I saw Malik. He was standing tall, arms crossed, and his gaze was locked on me like an anchor. When our eyes met, he nodded. Just once, but it was enough.

I exhaled slowly. "A lot. I was hurt. And I was angry. Really freaking angry. But, more than anything, I felt... used. Like I could just be cast aside when it was convenient. That feeling turned me into a different version of myself and made me reckless."

"Do you regret it?"

"Sometimes, but not really. In the moment, I thought they'd ruined my life. But really, they just ushered me to a different path," I said, catching his eyes again before looking back to Nadia.

"Would that path happen to include your boyfriend, Malik?" Nadia asked, her teasing smile as sharp as her too-perfect winged eyeliner.

"Yeah," I laughed, feeling my cheeks heat in a blush. "It would."

"He's been by your side through a lot of this. Wasn't he your getaway driver that night?" I startled and shook my head.

"I don't know how you found that out, but yes, he was," I replied, trying to smile through my shock.

"How did you meet him?"

Now, I really did laugh. Malik's eyes widened and he shook his head.

"Ibiza. We got matching tattoos," I said, waggling my eyebrows.

"Okay. Explain," she said, her eyes widening as she leaned forward.

"We were at a music festival. Malik was a traveling tattoo artist. I was there as a PA. I was on an absolutely crucial mission to find strawberries—don't ask. We chatted, he offered me a micro-tattoo, and when I got nervous, he tattooed himself first to show me it wasn't a big deal."

"That's insane! But it totally fits," she laughed. "Do we get to know what it is?"

Malik made a noise in the back of his throat, and everyone on set turned to look at him.

"I'm gonna say that's a no," I said. I gave Malik a wink as everyone on set laughed.

"And then you fell in love."

I felt my heart thudding and I looked from her to Malik. That strong and sure look had gone all soft the way it had when we were both fueled by tequila, and I thought about the way he'd kept me sane and been my rock all these years.

"And then I fell in love," I repeated softly, my voice trembling slightly at the edges. The words hung heavy between us, and for one fragile second, it felt like we were the only two people in the room. Any oxygen I had in my lungs was sucked out, and it was like that moment between us was frozen.

We were separated by space and camera equipment, but it was like his hand was back on my chin, tilting my face up to his gaze. I barely noticed a camera turning to point at him because I was studying the way his jaw went slack, and his hand rubbed at his chest like he felt the same ache that I did.

When I was able to pull my gaze away from his, I sucked in a breath like I'd forgotten how to breathe. "Malik is... everything. He is one of the few people who never looked at me like I was a punchline or a headline.

He was just... there. And he's still here, demolishing me at Scrabble every chance he gets."

Nadia's smile softened. "Sounds like someone pretty special."

"Yeah." My voice wavered just slightly, and I looked right at him again. "He is."

The conversation carried on. Some questions stung, and others felt like peeling off a scab. By the end of the hour, I felt hollowed out but... lighter. Like I'd put down a weight I hadn't realized I was still carrying. When the cameras finally stopped rolling, Nadia reached across the space between us and squeezed my hand.

"Thank you for your honesty, Cassia. Truly."

I nodded, unable to speak past the tightness in my throat.

Malik was waiting in the hallway, hands shoved into his pockets. The moment he saw me, his face split into a wide, easy grin.

"You did it," he said, his voice warm with pride.

"I did," I replied, beaming. "There's a dim sum spot nearby that's going to change your life," he said, slinging an arm around my shoulders with easy confidence as we walked out into the LA sun.

At that moment, everything felt real. No, more than that—it felt easy. Like, maybe we weren't pretending at all. And that made the world feel a little brighter.

Chapter 6

They'd finished editing the interview quickly, and it was up the next day. I approved it with no edits because I didn't manage to embarrass myself. According to these comments, I sold "well-adjusted and thriving" a little too much. The glow of my laptop screen lit up my face as I scrolled through an endless sea of notifications that all had one photo: Malik and me making eye contact when I said I'd loved him.

It wasn't even a dramatic photo, it was just... us.

Malik's face was soft as his eyes locked onto mine, his face raw and unguarded. And me? I looked like I was barely holding it together. Every emotion I'd been feeling since our almost kiss was written in big neon letters across my face.

I wasn't ready to dissect what that meant, but the internet had thoughts. A lot of thoughts:

> *HELLO?? Did anyone else feel that? Look at them! #RenegadeTamed*
>
> *She's in love?! But, I'm still single! I'm dying. Someone call an ambulance. #Redcarptetrenegade*
>
> *They did this whole interview and didn't kiss??? Cassia, please. I'm sick. #Cassilik*
>
> *I'm literally on my knees in the Walmart parking lot crying about the way Malik looks at Cassia. Someone sedate me. #RenegadeTamed*
>
> *If they don't get married, I'm suing Hollywood for emotional damage. #Redcarpetrenegade*

My stomach did a sick flip-flop thing every time I refreshed my feeds, and honestly, I didn't know if I was about to throw up or cry. I let out a strangled groan and threw my laptop down onto the couch.

"What?" Malik asked from his desk.

I grabbed a pillow and screamed into it before flopping back dramatically. "They think we're in love."

He froze, his eyes snapping to mine. "Oh."

"Oh? *Oh?*" I shot upright, running my hands through my hair like the over-caffeinated mad woman that I was. "Malik, they're making fan edits! There are random photos of us from years ago! Someone wrote *fanfiction!*"

He was trying—and failing—to hide his amusement as he raised his eyebrows. "What type of fanfiction?"

"Boy," I yelped, grabbing a towel from the couch and hitting him with it. "Do not read it. I can't believe this is happening," I moaned.

"Well, you did say you fell in love for everyone to hear," he said, typing at his computer.

"I was doing the whole smoke and mirrors thing," I said, waving my hands in frantic denial.

His cocky grin turned into a full beam as he looked at the screen. "Well, you really sold that smoke and mirrors. Oh, it's set in *MalInked,* and you're in an interesting position in my chair. I didn't think legs did that—"

Jumping up, I slammed his laptop shut and glared at him, growling, "What did I say?"

Malik leaned back in his seat, that same stupid smile on his face. This man was infuriatingly calm, and it made me want to strangle him. His tone was unworried as he asked, "Okay, so what do we do? Ignore it? Lean into it?"

"Lean into it?" I asked, my butt hitting his desk.

"Hey, it's not all bad. This? It's control. You're steering the narrative this time."

I sighed, letting his words sink in. He was right, in a way. After years of being the butt of the joke, the tabloid chaos, the memeable meltdown, I finally had a chance to redirect the spotlight. But that didn't mean it wasn't complicated.

"I just don't get it," I admitted, kicking my feet out in front of me. "Why are people so obsessed with this? It's fake."

Malik's whiskey-colored eyes met mine, steady and unreadable. "Because it doesn't *look* fake."

My stomach did a weird little swoop because he wasn't wrong. The weight of what he said settled over us. Tension simmered in the space between us, and I hated how warm it made me feel. How easy it would be to pretend. Pretend like I'm with him, like this lie is true.

"You're good at this," I said, trying to defuse the tension in the room. "Playing the perfect boyfriend."

"I've had years to practice." His grin was teasing, but there was a shadow of something behind it. A flicker I couldn't quite decipher, and then it was gone.

I rolled my eyes, fighting the urge to ask him about it. "Don't let it go to your head. This whole Hunk-ules thing is an act."

"Sure," he said, voice low, highlighting his southern drawl. "An act."

The air between us thickened again, the silence stretching. His gaze lingered, dark and steady, like he was daring me to challenge him. My eyes flittered down to his lips for the briefest of moments, and my insides got all soupy.

I cleared my throat, desperate to break whatever weird spell had settled over us. "We should probably post a photo," I said, holding up my phone. "Play into the hype. Keep people talking until the party."

He quirked an eyebrow and grabbed the phone from me. "I have an idea." He pressed a few buttons on my phone and propped it up, so it was facing the tattoo chair in the corner. "Come here," he said, standing and holding out his hand.

Looking back, I saw that the phone was recording. What was he up to? He plopped down into the tattoo chair. When I was close enough, he grabbed me and pulled me forward into his lap. I fell forward and he caught my weight easily.

His voice dropped teasingly, low enough to make my pulse trip over itself, as he leaned up toward my ear. "What should I whisper to make you blush?"

His hands on my waist dipped just beneath the seam of my shirt, his thumbs brushing along my skin, sending a shiver skittering up my spine.

"Or," his tone softened, a current of something deeper in it now. "I could just tell you the truth."

I froze.

He pulled back just enough to meet my eyes, his voice steady but quieter, was meant just for me. "You amaze me, Cass. Not just your beauty." His fingers tightened ever so slightly against my waist and sending my stomach into several somersaults. "But your strength—the way you keep trying, even when it hurts, even when the world's watching is—incredible. Because you are incredible. Any man would be lucky to have you."

I blinked. The room suddenly felt too small, far too hot. His gaze didn't waver, and for a second, I forgot how to breathe. This wasn't fake. Not right now. Not the way he was looking at me, like I was something to be treasured, something worth protecting.

I forced a laugh, shaky and thin. "The internet's gonna think you're actually in love with me."

His lips curved, just barely, his eyes never leaving mine. "Maybe I am."

The air felt like it had been sucked out of the room. My stomach dropped, my mouth went dry, and for a second, I was sure I misheard him. But then he winked, casual as ever, and the moment shattered.

"You're impossible," I groaned, pushing to my feet, he followed me up.

"I don't half-ass things," he replied, smug and smooth, as he reached for my phone and ended the recording. He pressed a few buttons, and I stared at him gob smacked as he cropped the beginning and end off the video before throwing sound underneath and typing while talking aloud, "*Fanfiction giving us ideas.* Posted. That should keep the internet talking."

My legs felt shaky, but I tried to ignore them. "Great," I said.

But even as I tried to keep my tone breezy, my mind was a whirlwind of questions I didn't dare ask. Like whether the way his hands lingered a moment too long, the way his voice softened when he said those words, meant something more.

I grabbed my phone and muttered a quick, "Thanks," before slipping out of the room. My chest felt tight as I made my way to the door, fumbling to regain my composure.

Behind me, I heard him chuckle, low and warm. "Anytime, Cass."

I stumbled out of the room, my pulse racing and my brain short-circuiting.

What was *that*?

Malik was playing his role too damn well, and my body was reacting like an idiot. My heart was thudding, and I was doing my best to not hyperventilate. When did Malik turn sexy? The man had been tattooing me for years, and never once had I felt the inferno of his touch before this all started.

The air outside felt cooler, but it didn't help much. It felt tight, like the walls were closing in on me. The noise of the shop was distant. I couldn't make eye contact with any of them, not with the way my face was flaming and my body was vibrating.

I clutched my phone tighter, shaking my head. Nope. This was fake. Malik was just being—Malik. Generous, supportive, annoyingly good at playing a swoon-worthy boyfriend. That's all it was.

But then, why did it feel like I was on the verge of setting myself on fire every time he got too close? A notification lit up my screen, snapping me out of my downward spiral. Another mention. Another tag. There was a flood of new comments under the video we'd just filmed. The clip hadn't been up for five minutes, and it was already spreading like wildfire.

THE WAY HE TOUCHES HER? HE'S DOWN BAD, Y'ALL. #Cassilik

What is he saying?! Can anyone read his lips? Please.

They're reading the fanfiction! When the girlies find out...

I groaned, shoving my phone into my pocket like that would somehow silence the internet. But the damage was done. Every comment, every like, every share—they all chipped away at the fragile wall I'd built around this whole fake dating charade.

It's not real. It's not real. It's not—

The door swung open, and Malik stepped out, casually stretching like he hadn't just turned my entire body into molten lava. His eyes landed on me, and his smile softened into something more careful.

"You okay?"

"Peachy," I lied, my voice too high-pitched to be convincing. "The internet's eating this up."

His gaze lingered for a beat longer, his expression unreadable. "Good," he said finally. "That's the point, right?"

"Right." I nodded, not even remotely believing myself.

I turned toward the bathroom, mumbling something about needing a minute. As soon as I was inside, I locked the door and slumped against it, my breath shaky.

My phone buzzed again, the video notifications multiplying. But I didn't check them. I couldn't. Instead, I stared at the ceiling and whispered to myself, "Get it together, Cassia. This is fake. He's just *really* good at pretending."

But the way my stomach flipped at the memory of his touch? Yeah. That felt anything but fake.

Christ on a cracker. This was not good.

Chapter 7

After the video heard round the world, I'd put all of my social media apps on mute. I barely touched them before this, and the attention from the video was intense and chaotic. I didn't know how anyone could deal with it every single day. My phone vibrated, and I had a small sliver of hope that it was someone asking me about being a PA.

The whole point of this was to get a job. Opening the notification, I realized it was a text from Jade.

You're not gonna believe this.

Groaning, I brought my gaze back up to my cracked ceiling. I was exhausted from all the attention and the tags and the questions. I don't know why I hadn't expected this. Deep down, I thought it would fly under the radar and stop the memes. But I just had to look at Malik with something vulnerable and open.

I opened the text and replied.

What now?

The phone rang and I begrudgingly answered it.

"You're on the guest list for the Pierro rooftop party tonight," she squealed. "A friend asked if I had the number for your agent to invite you."

"The Pier—my agent? I'm a PA, I'm not an influencer."

She shushed me and I flopped back onto my couch. "You are now."

"No. I'm not," I said.

She sighed, and I heard her tapping on her phone.

"You don't understand. Cassia. It's one of *the* parties of the year." Her line clicked. "Hold on," she said.

She came back, and I could hear the telltale buzz of a tattoo gun in the background.

"You snitched on me?" I moaned, fighting the urge to flop around on the floor like a toddler.

"Good morning to you too, sunshine. Pierro's is perfect," Malik said without missing a beat.

"Perfect? Malik, this isn't some casual hangout. These are real Hollywood people. Important people."

"And now they think you're important too. Hold on," The gun went quiet for a minute as he talked to his client about something. When the buzzing started up again, he hit me with, "You can't rewrite history if you don't take a chance. You're never going to have a moment like this one again."

"See, this is your moment! Get your ass in gear." Jade practically yelled into her phone. I opened my mouth to argue, but he wasn't wrong. The Pierro party was a legendary event. One that could launch a career—or revive one.

"I don't have anything to wear." It was my last ditch effort to stop the freight train this whole thing had become.

"Text me your size, I have a friend who would love to dress you. They'll messenger you over a bunch of looks."

Sighing, I begrudgingly said, "Fine. But if anyone brings up that fanfiction—"

"Have you read the new one on the beach in Ibiza?" Jade sounded way too excited about all of this.

"I'm hanging up now," I announced before disconnecting.

What was my life now?

I stood in front of the mirror, smoothing the sleek black fabric of my dress for the tenth time. Jade's friend made stunning clothes, but this ensemble was something else. It was fitted to perfection, with a plunging neckline and a slit up one side that stopped just past the point of scandalous. It hugged every curve without apology, the sheen of the fabric catching the light whenever I moved. I felt like I could conquer the world in this.

And that's exactly what I'd needed.

My makeup was bolder than usual—winged eyeliner, sharp as hell. I'd matched it with a red lip that screamed confidence. It was a fiercer version of what I'd worn on the red carpet that night, and it was intentional. I was still the same bitch, and I wanted to make sure that people knew that.

I'd left my hair in its natural wavy style, massaging and tossing the soft curls over my shoulders. And the heels? Still horrendous torture devices. But damn, they were doing everything they were meant to.

As much as I wanted to pretend like I was annoyed, I was excited. I looked good, I felt good, and I was going to stun tonight. If only I could get my heart to stop galloping every time I thought of a certain gorgeous tattooed man.

When I stepped outside, Malik was leaning against his motorcycle, scrolling through his phone. He was dressed in dark blue with a leather jacket over his dark shirt, with slim-fit pants that made his legs look unfairly long. Colorful tattoos peeked out from beneath the unbuttoned shirt. His boots, scuffed just enough to look intentional, added to the whole rugged-yet-refined aesthetic he'd somehow perfected.

He lowered his phone slowly as his dark eyes traced a leisurely path from my heels, over my body, and up to my face. His mouth parted slightly, like he was about to say something, but no words came out.

I resisted the urge to fidget under his gaze, my pulse doing its best impression of a jackhammer. "So?" I asked, trying to sound casual.

"You look..." He paused, his voice dropping a little, like he was fighting to find the right words. "Unbelievable."

My cheeks heated. "Thanks," I said, aiming for breezy but landing closer to breathless. "You clean up pretty well yourself."

His lips curved into a slow, knowing smile, and I felt my insides do the dancey thing that they'd been doing around him for the last week. "You're gonna have every eye in the room on you tonight."

I glanced at his shirt, then back to his face, unable to stop myself from appreciating how well it all fit together—the sharp lines, the effortless confidence, the way he smelled like cedar and something faintly spicy.

Seeing a piece of lint, I grabbed it, brushing off his jacket, my fingers tingling. "Good thing, you'll be there to scare them off," I quipped, trying to deflect away from the way my heart was thumping against my ribs.

His eyes became laser focused as they scanned my body once more. "Oh, I'll do more than that. Don't worry, Cass. You're in good hands."

Something about the way he said it, so smooth and certain, eased some of the fear coiling wildly in my stomach. I turned toward the waiting car, my heels clicking against the pavement. "Let's get this over with."

"Whatever you say, beautiful," he murmured, just loud enough for me to hear.

As the driver navigated the winding streets toward the rooftop, I couldn't stop replaying that moment in my head. The way his eyes had lingered, the way his voice had dropped, like he wasn't playing a part—like he really was stripping me down to the very fabric of my being with every gaze.

I stole a glance at him from the corner of my eye. He was scrolling through his phone, his expression unreadable, but his jaw looked tighter than usual. His free hand rested on his knee, the veins on his forearm just visible where his sleeve had pushed up.

This was a bad idea. A very bad idea. Because every time he looked at me like that, like I wasn't just his fake girlfriend but something more, it felt less and less like we were pretending.

The rooftop was magnificent.

We could see Hollywood Hills, all lit up and sprawling. LA was a truly magical place, with all its glittering lights and iconic features. I was never going to get over being able to call it home. But all these people—people that literally starred in movies—what the fuck was I doing here? Malik sensed the unease I felt as we stepped off the elevator and offered me his arm. After a second of hesitation, I took it.

"Relax," he murmured as we stepped sideways into the corner. When he leaned closer to me, his musky scent surrounded me.

"Where's that bad bitch?" he asked. He spoke right into my ear.

"Here," I whispered.

He gave me a look like he didn't believe me as he lightly brushed my lip with his thumb. My breath stuttered in my chest.

"Nah. Close your eyes," he said. "Take two big breaths."

I did, shutting them tight and gripping his arm with my other hand.

"Now look at me."

Opening my eyes, his nose was dangerously close to mine. His fingers found my jaw and awareness heated my body.

"Where is the Renegade?" he asked again.

The way he said it, it wasn't a question. It was a demand, a reminder of who I'd been before the world turned me into a punchline. I felt something rising in me. Pride or defiance—or maybe both?

"Right fucking here," I replied.

"She sure the hell is. Now come on. Let's go put on a show." He kissed my cheek before pulling away and pasting a blank look on his face that screamed mysterious.

I smiled wide and scanned the room, catching a few people who watched our little moment. Nodding at them, I let Malik walk me into the lion's den.

The crowd parted for us in a way that felt almost cinematic. Heads turned, whispers trailed behind us, and for the first time in years, the attention didn't feel like judgment. It felt like curiosity. Admiration, even.

A tall, statuesque, woman I immediately recognized approached us with a flute of champagne in hand. Rosemary Ray was in the background of every event that took place in Hollywood. Well, every event but mine.

"Cassia James," she said, her voice honeyed and sharp. "And this must be Malik."

Malik extended a hand, his smile disarming. "That's me."

"You two are quite the pair," she said, her eyes flicking between us. "So... authentic. It's refreshing."

I forced a smile, trying not to let the word authentic make me choke. "We try," I barely managed to say.

"I'd love to attend your party later this week," she said.

"Of course. Consider your name added to the list," I breathed.

"Good, I'll see you then. Have a fabulous evening." She lingered for a moment longer before drifting away.

Well, hell.

As the evening wore on, I was getting better at playing my part. Smiling, laughing and leaning into Malik. I wasn't just selling the illusion, I was embracing it. When people asked about us, I was honest. He was the most important person to me. We spent a lot of time together. There were inside jokes between the both of us that made us look at each other and hide in our drinks.

And Malik, the man was working magic as he remained mysterious and serious. He hadn't given a belly laugh that led to that little giggle all night. He was perfect. Too perfect. After two hours, I was taking a breather, hiding at the edge of the terrace.

He'd just gone on the hunt for alcohol. I'd been so nervous before that I thought I was gonna hurl, so I declined one. But Malik had talked me into a glass of Chardonnay now that I was feeling more comfortable.

He walked up behind me, his hand finding my waist as he leaned close behind me. "You're magnificent. Truly."

"Thanks to you," I said. "Seriously, how are you so good at this?" I was looking out at the city as I sipped the wine.

"At what?" he whispered.

"This. Us." I tried to turn, but he pulled my back against his front.

"I told you," he said quietly. "I don't half-ass things."

"Thank you for being in this with me," I whispered.

I wasn't sure he'd heard me as the silence stretched between us.

"Thank you for your vulnerability," he said just as low.

We sat in a companionable silence, listening to the party behind us, until someone called out his name. Malik straightened and he let me go. When I turned to him, he was pinning me with a scalding gaze that spoke volumes. He nuzzled my neck for a moment before his expression slipped back into his aloof mask as he waved back at the man.

"Brett." He strode away, but not before giving me one final glance over his shoulder.

The car ride home was quiet. We sat in the back, the space between us feeling small. Tension surrounded us, and I was doing my best to keep my attention on the building passing out the window and not on the tingling of my skin. He was watching me, waiting for me to look at him. I couldn't. If I did, I'd see that look he'd given me on the roof. And I didn't know if I could take the reminder that this was spiraling out of control.

I kept my eyes on the city lights outside the window, pretending not to notice the weight of his gaze until I couldn't take it. When I finally glanced over, his eyes were already on me, dark and searching. My breath hitched, and I turned back to the window, heart pounding.

As we finally pulled up to my apartment, I reached for the door and Malik reached across from me and gently pulled my hand from the latch.

"Let me," he said, stepping out. He shook our driver's hand and walked around the car and opened the door for me, holding a hand out to me. It was warm as I let him help me out. His gaze dropped to my feet.

"I won't keep you, I'm sure you're ready to throw those shoes in the trash."

I let out a cackle as I leaned against his shoulder, "If someone wasn't coming for them in the morning, they'd already be in there," I said through my laughter.

"Here," he said, helping me to the front of my building. "I can help you up," he offered.

"I am okay." I said, taking two steps and turning to face him. The tension between us continued to rise as I finally looked him in the eye. "Thanks for tonight," I said softly.

His expression was unreadable. "Anytime."

I leaned forward and found his cheek with my lips. It was soft and warm, and my eyes drifted as I inhaled the scent of him. His fingers grabbed my waist, burning a trail across my skin beneath my dress.

Slowly, I pulled back. His gaze locked onto mine, and for a fleeting moment, the world outside the dimly lit apartment entrance disappeared. I didn't want to step away, didn't want to break whatever spell had wrapped itself around us. But then he drew in a breath, his fingers brushing my waist one last time before retreating, leaving a cooling trail in their wake.

"Go get some sleep. You have a long day tomorrow."

I smiled at him as I took each step carefully, waving at him as the door shut behind me. My phone buzzed with a new notification. Another photo. Another wave of comments. But I didn't give a damn about any of that because the only thing I could think of was kissing my only friend.

This was supposed to be fake, but every day, every interaction sank me deeper into a new reality I didn't know how to navigate.

Chapter 8

I had my heat on—yay, money!—as I sat in my living room, thinking about the sheer chaos that the last few years had brought to my life. All my social media apps were back on silent as I listened to my version of meditation music: early 2000s pop-punk. As the heavy guitar and screamo filled the room, I let my eyes drift shut. Song after song played, but my mind was still a jumbled mess beneath the chords.

It wasn't just the feeling I had when I found out about Shrek and Fiona. Nor was it cursing him out in a local coffee shop when we met up to give him back his stuff. It wasn't even about Malik and that stupid, stupid look he'd given me in the viral photo.

It was our friendship.

Every memory of him was suddenly playing on a loop in my head—his tattoos glinting against his skin under the Ibiza sun, the way his smile had knocked the wind out of me at the grocery store, the countless nights I'd spent venting to him while he sketched designs for my next tattoo.

All of the ink on my body came from his brain, straight to my skin. I'd tell every person about his insane attention to detail when they saw the vibrant colors on my brown skin. No one could tattoo like he could. But he wasn't just my tattoo artist. He wasn't just my friend.

He was... everything.

And that scared the hell out of me.

If I lost him, I wouldn't just be losing my friend, I'd be losing the one person who had seen me, who had made me feel like I was worth seeing.

So, whatever this was, I had to cut it out. I wasn't willing to risk losing him because my hormones decided to suddenly recognize him as a human male. Plus, what if I'd imagined the whole thing? He could just be that good at playing the role I'd asked him to play, and I was just getting lost in the illusion.

I could already see the train wreck: Malik pulling away, me left to pick up the shattered pieces of whatever this was, pretending like I wasn't gutted every time I saw him.

Groaning, I buried my face in my hands. This wasn't supposed to happen. I wasn't supposed to feel... anything anymore.

Not like this. Not about Malik.

Every time he looked at me, smiled at me, or touched my hand, it felt like I was a speeding train hurtling toward a brick wall. I couldn't stop, and I couldn't steer. I could only watch as it got closer, the weight of what I might lose pressing down on me.

The venue was gorgeous—on paper. In reality, it looked like a post-apocalyptic prom night. The red-and-black streamers hung limp in the damp air, half of the rented lights were stuck on a flickering blue, and the sound tech was nowhere to be found.

I was going to find whoever was responsible for this atrocity and visit every single person who had ever met them and rain down pain and strife.

My clipboard trembled in my hand as I scanned the chaos, biting the inside of my cheek to keep from screaming.

"You're good," I whispered to myself, surveying the cavernous space. "This is fine. You can fix this."

Karina, the event planner for the space, appeared beside me, tablet in hand, her expression tight. "So... two things," she began cautiously, her tone apologetic. "The florists are running behind because their truck broke down, and they're asking if you want to change the delivery location. Also, the photographer said something about needing a better 'vibe' and left to scout a 'grungier aesthetic.' Whatever that means. Oh, and we're sold out."

I blinked, my mind reeling. "The vibe is the vibe," I snapped, waving a hand at the room. "Ho-How—"

My phone buzzed violently in my pocket, and I yanked it out to see three missed calls from the DJ and a text from him quitting. Fantastic.

"I'll fix it," I muttered, half to Karina, half to myself. "I'll fix everything." But my breath shallow, my lungs tightening. I shoved the clipboard into Karina's hands and stumbled toward the exit, muttering something about needing air.

Once outside, I collapsed into the driver's seat of my car, gripping the steering wheel so hard my knuckles turned white. My chest heaved as I stared blankly at the dashboard.

Breathe. Just breathe.

I fumbled for my phone and dialed the one person who always had answers.

"Cass?" Malik's voice came through rough with concern as he answered on the second ring.

"The florists are stranded, the photographer bailed, there's no DJ, and I think I might be having a heart attack."

There was a pause, and I imagined him frowning. "Okay, first, you're not having a heart attack. Second, florists and photographers are fixable. Take a deep breath."

I inhaled shakily, clutching the phone like a lifeline. "I don't even know where to start."

"Leave it to me," he said, his tone so calm it almost made me believe him. "I know a guy who can tow the florist's truck, my homeboy Francis is a DJ, and I'll call the guy who does my event photography. They're solid."

"You 'know a guy,'" I echoed weakly, disbelief coating every word.

"I know lots of guys," he said, and I could hear the faint laughter in his voice. "Now stop spiraling, send me the details, and swing by the shop later, we'll have dinner and talk through the rest."

I let out a breath, my grip on the wheel loosening slightly. "You're annoyingly good at things."

"Cass, you are brilliant. And you've got this. Let me handle this so you can focus on the rest."

When I hung up, I had a renewed sense of purpose. I slammed my car door and took another big breath before walking back into the shitshow that would be a party in less than twenty-four hours.

The first thing I did was waltz right back into the venue and start barking orders, "Alright. Take all these streamers down, I don't need anyone being reminded of the night they didn't lose their virginity. All these tables are in the wrong configuration. I also need someone to make a run to all the stores in the area. I'm going to make a list of what we need. They want Cass and Malik, they're gonna get it."

Everyone started to run around, and I smiled for the first time, that day. Maybe this would be okay. It had to be.

Malik was leaning over his station, sketching with a precision that always seemed otherworldly. He looked up as the door shut, a small smile tugging at his lips.

"Hey, feeling better?"

I rolled my eyes but couldn't help the faint smile that crept onto my face. "Barely. Hey Josephine," I said, waving at the blonde who literally was covered head to toe in ink.

"Hey girl!" she shouted.

"You saved my ass. Again," I said once I got closer to him.

"Just doing my job," he said lightly, but the warmth in his eyes betrayed something deeper. "Come on, I got us Chinese for dinner."

I clapped and jumped, "Oh, chow mein makes me do something strange."

He froze, slowly turning to look me up and down. "Please, never utter that sentence again."

I rolled my eyes and pushed him out of the way. "Whatever, Howie Mandel."

"I had the soul patch for three months. We don't talk about that time you got those short ass bangs."

I whirled on him, hissing, "That was the stylist. And I haven't gotten a haircut since because it was traumatic. You chose to get that shit smear on your face. Not. The.

Same." Poking his chest for emphasis, I watched as his eyes lit up.

"There she is," he whispered.

Narrowing my eyes, I shook my head and pushed open the door to his office. "You know I'm hangry, why are you pushing my buttons?"

"I like pushing your buttons," he said, wiggling his eyebrows at me.

I sank onto the couch, the tension finally bleeding out of my shoulders as they eased into the rest of our usual dynamic—shared takeout, quiet moments, and unspoken tension simmering beneath the surface.

It was two in the morning, and we were still sitting on his office couch, two half-eaten boxes of Chinese takeout sat on the coffee table. The rest of the shop was empty, and we probably should've already headed home, but we'd been deep in conversation as he moved his pencil across his sketch pad.

The party was tomorrow. I needed to go home and get some sleep, but I didn't want to. Something about being in the moment with him made me comfortable and I wasn't ready to give that up just yet.

I was staring over his shoulder, and he was sketching, deftly shading the intricate lines of a new design. I couldn't stop staring at the lines crisscrossing each fingers, at the veins that ran along the backs of his hands, at the way his pen moved so effortlessly across the paper, creating exactly what was in his head.

"You're staring," he said without looking up, a teasing lilt in his voice.

"No, I'm not," I shot back, grabbing a piece of cold chicken and shoving it into my mouth.

He grinned, finally glancing at me. "What's going on in that head of yours, Cass?"

I hesitated, the words caught in my throat. But then I remembered the way he'd looked at me in that photo, the raw honesty in his eyes. He deserved seeing that in mine too.

"What if this—" I gestured vaguely between us, "—gets messed up? What if we ruin everything?"

Malik set down his sketchpad, his expression softening. "What makes you think we will?"

"Because that's what always happens," I said, my voice barely above a whisper. "People leave, or things change, and suddenly nothing's the same anymore."

He leaned forward, his eyes steady on mine. "Cass, I'm not going anywhere."

The certainty in his voice made my chest ache. But it also terrified me because promises like that always came with an expiration date.

I didn't reply. What could I say? Only the hum of the ceiling fan filled the space as I leaned back against the couch and tried to focus on his words and not my apprehension.

"You ever think about why we do this?" he turned his head to look at me, his brown eyes unusually soft. "Why we hide from people, especially when those people matter?"

My heart thudded in my chest. "I—I don't know."

He hesitated, tapping his pen against the sketchpad as his fingers fidgeting. "It's almost easier to play the part," he said, his voice quieter now. "To pretend you don't want more when the risk feels too big." He let out a quiet laugh, shaking his head.

"More?" I echoed, my voice barely audible.

His fingers tightened around the edge of the sketchpad, a telltale sign he was holding back something. When his gaze held mine, I could almost see the war he was waging in himself. For a moment, I thought he was going to say something, but he looked away.

"Nah, forget I said anything," he muttered, picking up his sketchpad again.

I couldn't.

The weight of his words settled on me, heavier than I was ready to carry. He might have brushed it off, but the way he'd looked at me, so raw and unguarded, said everything he wouldn't. What if he wasn't just talking about pretending for the world? What if he was talking about... us?

I opened my mouth to say something—anything—but the words tangled with each other in my throat. What if I shattered this fragile moment we'd built, and he didn't mean what I thought? What if I was wrong?

The silence stretched between us, heavy and crackling with unspoken words. I needed to ask what he meant, but the courage drained away. And all I could do was sit there, the questions still pressing against my chest, unspoken and unrelenting.

Chapter 9

I sat on the couch in my bra and panties, staring at the dress draped over the back of my chair. It was a stunning fire engine red, and it wrapped tight around my waist, ending right below my ass cheeks. It screamed powerful, untouchable bad bitch, everything I needed to feel tonight. And that vibe was precisely what I needed because I wasn't feeling that way.

Everything I'd done was to rehabilitate my career. But, even now, all I got was questions about collaborations and appearances. I'd been thinking about it and maybe that wasn't a bad thing. There wasn't much I particularly liked about being a PA. What if that was the better path? I took a breath and looked over at the dress again.

It wasn't the time for another doom spiral. It was showtime. And that meant that I was gonna hike up my big girl thong and put on this dress and get it to fucking together. Because this was it.

Standing up, I took a deep breath.

I grabbed the dress off the couch and shimmied it up and over my thighs, past my hips and rolls and up over my arms. I looked in the mirror, watching the way the fabric clung to me. The last two years, I'd shown up in jeans and a t-shirt on purpose. My fingers traced the fabric, and I smiled.

It wasn't me.

At all.

At all, at all. But if all eyes were going to be on me, anyway, might as well give them something gorgeous to look at.

The venue was a hive of activity when I arrived through the back, clipboard in hand and a mask of composure firmly in place. Inside, it was chaos—vendors scrambling to set up, assistants running around inside, fussing over lighting, and staff running around like they were on fire. My stomach churned, but I shoved the panic down and barked orders like my life depended on it. Everything inside was almost complete, and my new section outside was ready to be unveiled.

Everything was starting to come together when Malik walked in.

He was dressed in a sleek blazer and dark jeans, his usual effortless cool turned up to eleven. His eyes swept the room before landing on me, and the soft smile that tugged at his lips sent an annoying warmth spreading through my chest.

God, the things I wanted to do to that man.

Focus, Cass.

"You're late," I said, trying to sound stern as I looked around behind him and counted the tables for the eighteenth time. Straightening the speech on my clipboard, I looked up at him. His gaze skimmed over my belted coat.

"No, I'm not. And you're absolutely delectable," he replied, bringing his lips to my neck and kissing right beneath my ear. My tummy flipped and flopped, and I felt the heat growing between my thighs.

"I-I'm not even wearing makeup. And you can barely see my dress, liar." I ignored the fact that my voice went up half an octave as I stuttered like a weirdo.

"I like what I do see," he whispered, grazing the edge of my jacket above my peeking breasts before pulling away.

"Is this the only black you have left in your wardrobe?" I asked, trying to tell myself that he was putting on a show for the room.

He rolled his eyes, "Now you know I look good."

"You do," I agreed, taking him in one more time, toes to head.

"Now, tell me what I need to do before they open the doors," he said.

"I need to check with the bartenders, and then we need to make sure security is strict about the count. We sold so many tickets, I have a feeling it's gonna be a shitshow, outs—"

"And you need to do your makeup. And hair."

"And I need to do my makeup and hair," I agreed, wiping sweat from my face, touching the scarf secured to my head.

"Okay. Bartender, security. And I see your coordinator over there, I'll go check in with her. You go," he said, pushing me towards the back room.

"I—"

"Trust me. I got it," he whispered, in my ear, making me want to do some very unspeakable things.

"I—"

"Cassia Calliope James. Take your ass in that room and get ready. I'll come get you when it's time."

Glaring at his tone, I watched as he looked down at me like he was ready for me to argue with him. His eyebrow raised as he blocked the door back into the venue, and I glared at him.

I hated how easily he made everything feel manageable. But I didn't have space to dwell on how he made me feel safe, there was too much to do, and I needed to start with really getting myself together.

I was staring at myself in the mirror, ready as I was ever going to be. I was showing more breasts and thighs than a grocery store, but I looked good as hell. My curls were artfully pinned at the top of my head, and my makeup was giving 90s natural. I didn't want to overshadow the dress. It wasn't the Cass that everyone expected, and that's why it was perfect.

The sound of glasses clinking and chatter drifted down the hall towards me, as my stomach pitched. It was my eighth time reading through my speech when I heard a knock on the door.

"Come in," I said, my back to the door. I grabbed what I needed and looked down at the small speech I'd written. "Should I read from the paper. No, I shouldn't, I can remember it. I just want to get the words right. Man, I could really go for a really good filet right now. Medium rare. From that place on Santa Monica Boulevard. And... why aren't you—"

I turned to see Malik taking up the whole doorway with his body. His jaw was practically on the floor, but that's not what stole the air from my lungs. It was the storm brewing behind his eyes. This wasn't a cute, stolen glance, he was looking at me like I was a buffet, and he'd just finished a yearlong fast.

Electricity pulsed between us, and it was so thick, I could barely breathe. It was the answer to the question I'd been far too afraid to ask. He felt the same way that I did.

"Mal—"

"Shh." The word was barely audible, but I heard it. It carried so much promise that it almost made my legs shake. And that's right where his attention went. Up from my ankles, to my calves, and pausing on my exposed thighs. Then, he moved from my hips up past my belly to my breasts, his teeth finding their way into his bottom lip. It was like his gaze was burning a hot trail straight through me, and every part of me was aflame.

When he finally met my eyes, I was breathing hard, and he looked ready to rip my dress off. And I wanted him to.

"I thought." I cleared my throat, "it was all for the cameras," I forced out.

He raised an eyebrow but didn't say a word, just held out his hand and looked at me expectedly. My heart was beating too hard. I couldn't think. Not with the way he was looking at me and clouding my thoughts.

And he looked so good. The blazer was open, and he'd left five buttons undone, showing his complex tattoos that danced vibrantly across his dark skin.

"The plan for the night is going to change if I have to come in there for you." His tone was playful, but I knew he was serious by the way he licked his lips.

After one unsteady step and then another, I reached his hand. Its soft heat enveloped mine as he pulled me close.

His lips came to my cheek softly before he traced a fiery trail to my ear, whispering, "You're absolutely fucking edible in this dress." His tongue reached out to find my earlobe, sucking my flesh into his mouth. My body was so slick, I was going to have to find a spare minute to throw my panties away.

I was sure my eye was twitching as I tried to breathe through the chaos playing across my nerves. Because Malik wanted me. Like, really wanted me. And the very thought made me want to both burst into happy tears and fall to my knees like I was in a porno, so I could swallow his anaconda whole. When I tried to slow down my steps and process what was going through my brain, he pulled me gently along beside him.

A security guard opened the doors for us, and we strode inside. The cameras were right there, following us as I headed over to the raised platform and the DJ turned the music down. Once people saw me, the room erupted in hoots and hollers as the hundreds of people filling the space looked at me.

Malik kissed my cheek and sidestepped over to the edge of the stage, leaving me in front of the mic. I let things die down a bit before I said, "Welcome to Love Me Not 3!"

The room went wild again, and I laughed, looking over at Malik, who wasn't watching the crowd, he was watching me. I gave him a small nod, taking comfort in his presence.

"A little over three years ago, something happened that changed my life, and I pulled together a party in two weeks to give love the finger. These parties have become more than that. As you move through each station, remember tonight is about you finding joy. And, I have a little surprise for you. To celebrate one of those new changes, you'll find something on the terrace: Scrabble! Each board is missing L, O, V, and E. Now, as per tradition, please hold up your paper hearts." I put mine over my head. The room followed suit.

"Love me," I cried out.

"Love me not," they echoed back, tearing their hearts.

Malik's eyes smiled as he came towards me and the crowd buzzed with excitement. Phones were out, recording every moment, and the chatter got louder as he moved closer.

"Come on, kiss her!" someone shouted.

The room exploded with cheers. The chants grew louder, reverberating through the room like a pulse.

"Kiss! Kiss! Kiss!"

They wanted a show. Hell, they demanded it. I stood frozen, my heart hammering against my ribs.

"Cass," he murmured, his voice low and warm as his hand found mine. His thumb brushed over my knuckles, the gentle, rhythmic stroke unraveling the tight coil of nerves in my chest.

I looked up at him. The world tilted, the room blurred, the noise dulled, and it was just—us. Malik's hand anchored mine as his shining brown eyes searched my face. His look was filled with something raw and unspoken. The air between us felt electric, a live wire humming with possibilities.

I leaned in, so slowly it felt like the air itself was frozen in time.

My lips brushed his, a soft and featherlight touch that sent a shiver rippling through me. That's when my world cracked open. Every nerve ending in my body fired at once, sparking with the force of life itself. I moaned in surprise as he deepened the kiss.

His hand slid to the curve of my waist, his fingers curling around me like he was afraid I'd slip away. Warm and firm lips moved against mine with a confidence that stole my breath. My hands reached their way to his chest, the fabric of his blazer soft beneath my fingertips, and I clung to him like he was the only thing keeping me tethered to the universe.

It wasn't just a kiss. It was a detonation. A starburst. It burned through every doubt, every fear, every carefully constructed wall I'd built around myself. His tongue brushed mine, and I tasted him—mint and something deeper, richer. My knees buckled, and he held me tighter, his arm a steady anchor around my waist.

Time fractured. I forgot about the crowd, the cameras, the party. There was only Malik, the way his lips moved against mine, the way his hand splayed across my lower back, pulling me impossibly closer. It felt like falling and flying at the same time, and I didn't want it to end.

When I finally pulled back, gasping for air, my head was spinning, my heart thundering so loudly I could barely hear the cheers erupting around us.

"Wow," I whispered, my voice trembling.

His eyes were darker now, his gaze locked on mine with an intensity that made my breath hitch. "Not yet," he murmured, his voice rough and low.

And then he kissed me again.

This time it was slower, deeper, like he was pouring everything he wanted to say into my lips. His mouth moved against mine with a calculated tenderness, his fingers finding my nape, leaving a tingling trail in their wake. I felt like I was being unraveled and stitched back together, only to be pulled apart again. My hand moved and I savored the heat of his skin. The rush of my pulse thundered in my ears, as the steady thud of his heart beat beneath my palms.

When he finally pulled away, his forehead rested against mine. His breath was warm against my skin, and I swore I could feel the echo of his lips and tongue in every corner of my body. I wanted to kiss him forever. I wanted to get lost in him. I also wanted to find the nearest room so I could feel those gorgeous lips in all my other places.

My body was alive for the first time in a long time, and I wanted more.

I wanted, no—I needed—Malik.

His hand slid up to cup my cheek, his thumb brushing over my skin. His lips were moving, but I couldn't hear him.

I blinked, struggling to find words, to find air. "I..." My voice wavered as the sound in the room came back to life. The roaring was deafening, and I could feel the heat growing in my cheeks. I took a shaky breath as my hand found his cheek. His lips touched the inside of my palm and he held it to his face, and I was surprised I wasn't a messy pool of cum, sweat, and hormones right there on the floor.

We sat in that moment together for a second. If he was surprised by what had just happened, he wasn't showing it. He was giving me a smoldering look as I breathed hard and tried to convince my body to calm down.

"Wow," I repeated. He read my lips and gave me a wide smile. His thumb came to my chin, and he turned my head to look out at the crowd that was currently going bananas in front of us. I gave a little wave followed by a curtsy.

Malik brought his front to my back, and I felt his laughter rumbling in his chest. I smiled because I loved making that man laugh.

My body was still reeling and everything was finally coming into focus as I saw the event planner chasing behind someone.

Fiona Lane was walking into my party, and Shrek was by her side.

Chapter 10

The dizziness from Malik's kiss was making everything around me feel fuzzy. It took everything in me not to touch my lips, which still tingled like they'd been branded. My body hummed, every nerve on edge, and it was impossible not to imagine the thousand ways that kiss could've gone further. His arms, strong and steady, had left a phantom warmth that made me want to dive right back into them.

I really wanted to enjoy how alive I felt, how soaked my panties were from only his tongue in my mouth and maybe touch one of my painfully hard nipples.

But I had to deal with this bitch.

Fiona swept into the room with an entrance that screamed look at me. Her arm was hooked through Shrek's, and she had a sneer on her face like she'd just won a prize. The event coordinator flitted nervously beside her, attempting to stop their forward march, but Fiona brushed her off. I made eye contact with the event planner and shook my head.

It was too late to stop Fiona. If I'd been thinking, I'd have expected some bullshit like this. She'd been swearing up and down on social media that she didn't steal Shrek and that he'd left me, but no one was buying the lie. Of course, her silly ass would show up here.

A ripple of whispers cut through the crowd, heads turning as people noticed her.

"Is that Fiona Lane?" someone near me asked on a whisper.

"Oh my God, look what she's wearing," another muttered.

The dress was a monstrosity. Layers of ruffles cascaded around her like some kind of fashion catastrophe. And it absolutely was a catastrophe because the blinding lime green was so loud it could've doubled as a hazard sign. It clashed horribly with her skin, making her look washed out and sickly. She strutted like she was on a catwalk, her grin wide and self-assured.

"She's auditioning for *Little Bo Peep: The Musical,* clearly," Jade said as she materialized beside the stage, cocktail in hand. Her voice was low enough for only me to hear and I had to bite back a laugh. There were cameras, after all.

It felt good to have her in my corner and Malik at my back. I had a feeling I was going to need all my strength not to go full nuclear bomb on the silly bitch.

The room went dead quiet as everyone looked between Fiona and me. The crowd parted to give her and her hideous wardrobe space to walk. Fiona twirled dramatically, as if she hadn't heard the crowd's snickers.

"Cassia, darling!" Her voice was loud and syrupy, dripping with faux sweetness. "What a stunning party! I just had to come."

I forced a polite smile as Malik's arm fell across my body, its weight comfortable as he pulled me into him.

"Fiona. What a surprise," I said, not even putting any effort into pretending I wanted her there.

"Oh, I couldn't miss it," she gushed, loud and theatrical. "And I *had* to share the news. Look!" she thrust her hand forward, practically shoving it into my face. An enormous, ostentatious, ring caught the light. "We're engaged! Isn't it just perfect?"

The crowd's attention zeroed in on her announcement, but instead of the adoration she clearly expected, the reactions were... less than kind.

"Is that a ring or a paperweight?"

Another voice chimed in, "Looks like cubic zirconia to me."

I snickered before I could stop myself. The crowd's murmurs grew louder, and Fiona's smile faltered for just a moment before she recovered, her grin sharpening.

"I guess not everyone can appreciate elegance." She stepped forward, pulling Shrek along with her. "Cass," she said, leaning in conspiratorially. "It must be so hard for you to see me so... happy." Her voice was quiet enough that the crowd couldn't hear.

"Good for you," I said simply, refusing to rise to her bait.

Her eyes narrowed, and she spoke louder, her voice cutting. "You know, it's funny. You throw this party, put on this whole show, but all anyone's talking about is me. No matter how hard you try, Cass, you'll always be the girl who lost it." Her words were sharp as she spoke louder.

I met her gaze steadily, refusing to flinch. "If that's what you need to believe, Fiona," I said evenly, my tone devoid of the reaction she clearly craved.

Her composure cracked, just slightly, as she stared at me. Instead, I smiled faintly, a hint of amusement in my expression, as my fingers entwined themselves with Malik's. His thumb brushed against my knuckles in silent reassurance, and I turned and gave him a soft smile.

If you'd asked me how I'd have reacted a few days ago to seeing Fiona again, I probably would've gone with violent. But right at that moment, all I wanted was to enjoy the party, and get another one of those juicy kisses that sent me straight past Pluto. Around us, the crowd was watching intently, their amusement thinly veiled.

"How embarrassing," someone called out, followed by a thunder of laughter from the crowd.

Fiona's composure started to slip. Her voice rose, shrill and frantic. "You think you're so above it all, don't you? Everyone here knows you're a washed-up nobody pretending to be important!"

Jade sipped a cocktail and put a hand out in concern. "Daddy. Daddy, chill." The room erupted into laughter as Shrek's face turned a bright, splotchy red.

Fiona's eyes snapped to Jade, blazing with fury. "You think you're funny, don't you?" she hissed.

"Actually, I think I'm hilarious," Jade replied with a grin.

The crowd roared as Fiona continued to crumble. She whirled back to me, her voice sharp and frantic. "Everyone here knows you're a washed-up ugly, fat bitch!"

I stepped forward, my voice steady and calm. "Fiona, I think it's time for you to leave."

Her face twisted with rage. "I'm not going anywhere. I bought tickets! I have every right to be here!"

"You also have every right to act like an adult," I said calmly. "But clearly, that's asking too much."

Malik's arm tightened around my chest as he chuckled softly. "Cass, you're too kind," he murmured in my ear. "Fuck her."

I turned to the nearest security guard and nodded. "Please escort this Barbie looking bitch and her... guest the fuck out of my party."

Her eyes snapped to mine, wild and desperate. "You can't do that. I purchased tickets. I'm *allowed* to be here!"

Security moved towards them.

Shrek took a step back, his face beet red. "My name isn't Shrek. It's Chris." His voice went up an octave as he yelled to the crowd, shaking off Fiona's claws that had dug into his arm. "Stop calling me Shrek. It's not funny!"

As the guards approached, Fiona completely lost it. "I won!" When one grabbed her arm, she screamed in the lady's face, "I am a paying customer. I will sue you. Don't touch me—" Her voice was drowned out by the crowd, who booed and heckled loudly as the guards pushed her away.

The crowd erupted into cheers and applause as Fiona screamed incoherently, her voice inaudible over them.

"Don't let the door hit you!" someone shouted, followed by another round of cheers.

The room buzzed with renewed energy as Fiona disappeared out the door, Shrek bringing up the rear, still screaming about his name.

Jade turned to us where we still stood on the stage and gave the most satiated sigh I'd ever heard. Her grin was devious as she clapped gleefully. "That was *chef's kiss*. That made my whole month."

"Are you okay?" Malik asked in my ear. I turned and caught his gaze. He looked concerned, but all I felt was... relief. My hand traced the skin of his neck, and I nodded.

"I'm fine," I said, exhaling slowly. "It was... inevitable. But, I'm good."

"To Cassia motherfucking James, our unflappable resident bad bitch!" Jade shouted, raising her glass. The crowd erupted in laughter and cheers, clinking glasses in my honor.

"Let's fucking party!" I yelled.

Everyone roared and applauded as I let myself smile—really smile. The moment was mine, Fiona's shadow was banished for good.

Chapter 11

The party was alive in a way that only came when the drama had ended, and relief buzzed in the air like a lively hive of bees. And baby, was the hive getting down. After Fiona's exit, the mood had shifted into full celebration mode. Laughter echoed off the walls, glasses clinked, and the DJ's upbeat playlist kept people swaying.

It was me, I was swaying and living my best life.

Jade ushered me over to the bar and got me a shot. Now I was standing near her with a cocktail in hand, the fizzy pink concoction sparkling like everything else around me. My lips were still buzzing from the way that Malik's kiss fully devoured them, and every so often, I found him across the room, laughing with a group of guests. The way his smile stretched across his face sent shivers through me.

God, he was so... alive.

"This is the best party yet," Jade said, as she bumped my shoulder. She had a glass of something bright and citrusy in hand and a face that screamed mischief. "And I'm not just saying that because Fiona had the tantrum of the century."

I grinned. "She really gave us a show, didn't she?"

Jade snorted. "Understatement of the year. Did you hear someone call her dress a weapon of mass destruction? Iconic." She caught my gaze moving to Malik and scooted in front of me, blocking my view.

"So," Jade said, sipping her cocktail with a very demure look in her eyes.

I rolled my eyes and took a drink from my own, feeling the heat spread across my cheeks as my muscles relaxed.

"How are things?" she asked, raising her eyebrows.

"Jade."

"I just. I'm happy for you both. He's such a gentle soul. And you mean a lot to him," she said, touching my arm. "I see he means a lot to you too."

Scoffing, I turned my body, so I would stop staring in his direction, "He does," I said.

"You know," she said, as she leaned forward, and lowered her voice. "You aren't the same Renegade I met, your aura is different. You were giving a very disconnected and sad gray-white when we first met. I could see a hint of you underneath it, though. When you hit that stage, you were a healing greenish-orange. But after that kiss? Red. You were ready for him to wax the floor with you in front of all these people."

I snorted, feeling the alcohol going into my windpipe. Coughing, I did my best to clear the liquid from my throat. Jade smiled at me and nodded, not paying any attention to the fact that I was practically hacking up all of my insides in front of her.

"You're both super cute." she continued. "And in case you were wondering. His aura is always pink and green when you're around. Compassionate and nurturing. Loving."

If I wasn't already coughing my way into an early grave, I would be again as she gave me a sweet, knowing smile. I didn't reply, and she didn't look like she expected me to.

After a few minutes, I was outside on the terrace, sucking cold air into my lungs. It was so hot inside. Everyone came up to me and congratulated me on how well I'd handled Fiona, but I was starting to feel overwhelmed.

The crisp air was cutting through the fog in my brain when I smelled him—all smoky cedar and something warm.

"I was looking for you," he said, bringing his arms around me to the terrace.

"You found me," I whispered, knowing that folks were playing Scrabble around us. Instead of trying to pull away, I leaned into him, feeling his heat soak into my back.

"You made the party theme about us," he said, dragging his stubble against my neck, making me want to collapse and open my legs really, really wide.

"Well, we are the main attraction," I replied, trying my best not to shudder as pleasure rolled through me.

"I have an idea," he said, his lips nibbled my earlobe, and I could feel all the need I'd pushed aside start to coil in my stomach. "Think you can handle it, Cass?" his breath whispered past my ear, and the promise of his words were so filthy that I almost wanted to beg him to tell me more.

"Handle what?" I whispered.

"A game."

I shot him a look, the heat from his body, the things his tongue was doing, and the liquor made me bold. "Oh. You're seducing me as a distraction. I'm going to wipe the floor with you."

His grin widened, and I could tell he was enjoying this way too much. "Care to make it interesting?"

"Hmm. Continue."

Malik tilted his head, his eyes sparkling. "If I win, I get to plan tomorrow entirely my way. No arguments."

I raised an eyebrow, feeling a flicker of unease at the thought of what "his way" might entail. "And if I win?"

"Then it's your call," he said smoothly, as if he already knew he'd win. "Anything you want."

Yeah, he could beat me on a regular day, but playing with two less vowels? There was no way he wouldn't be thrown off by that. I turned fully in his arms, feeling the balcony at my back and the warm man at my front.

"Fine. But I've already had a few drinks. You have to catch up," I said, throwing up four fingers. I'd only had one drink. But I deserved a little bit of an edge, the man was a champion, after all. A cocky one, at that.

He signaled a girl carrying shots over and counted out four and placed them down near me. Then he grabbed two extras off the tray and handed one to me.

"Drink," he said, raising his eyebrow. Fine. Those four shots at once were going to give me the advantage that I needed. I could take another one.

"Fine. But don't cry when I beat you," I said, as I took the shot. The tequila burned in a bad way, and I was sad that I hadn't brought us a secret stash of the good stuff, but there would be time for that later, right now, we had a game to play.

The game descended into insanity almost immediately.

Removing the LOVE tiles may have been too much. O and E were two of the most commonly used letters in the English language, and without then we had ridiculous words that barely made sense. I managed to score a few points early on, but Malik was annoyingly good at finding obscure words that shouldn't have counted.

"You're making that up," I said, glaring at the board.

"*DHAYANA* is a word," he replied, feigning innocence. "Look it up."

"It is," someone chimed in near us. "It's a type of meditation."

We'd gained an audience somehow, and everyone was crowding around to see who would be victorious. The chalkboard at our table showed that I was seventy points behind, but I'd been behind worse.

"Meditate these nuts," I muttered under my breath.

Malik leaned forward, his breath brushing my ear. "Jealous of my vocabulary, Cass?"

I swallowed hard, pushing him back to his side of the table. "Hardly."

His attempt to rattle me was so obvious. I rolled my eyes. "Focus on the tiles, pretty boy. *SHIFTING.*"

The crowd gasped as I placed down all my tiles across two words, using a double letter and two triple words.

"That's one hundred and seventy-one points. Holy shit," someone said in awe.

I wiggled my eyebrows as he sat back in his seat and counted and recounted the points. He looked up at me, a question in his eyes. He wrote down the one hundred and seventy-one and stared at the board, trying to figure out how he was suddenly a hundred points behind.

Tapping my tiles, I watched in fascination as he calculated his next move.

The game wore on, with more laughter and arguments about made-up words, but he was taking it more seriously. When it finally came down to it, he was catching up.

As he looked at his tiles, I saw an opening to win the game. I stared at my tiles, trying to decide what to do. He was giving me that look that made his eyes twinkle and dance in the light.

Before I could second guess it, I said, "Pass."

He played the rest of his tiles and emerged victorious, grinning like a Cheshire cat. I groaned dramatically, slumping back in my chair as everyone around us laughed.

"Tomorrow's mine," he said smugly, leaning back in his chair.

As we stood, Malik grabbed my hand to interlace our fingers, but I tugged away from him, sticking out my tongue like a toddler. He pulled me gently, his hand firm around mine as he led me to the quiet corner. The dim alcove was tucked away from the hum of the party, illuminated by the faint glow of a string of fairy lights that flickered like stars. The laughter and chatter from the main room was muted, softened by the music and the steady thrum of my heartbeat.

I leaned against the cool wall, a contrast against the heat rushing through my body making me shiver. His gaze was locked on mine, his eyes unreadable but intense, and the space between us felt charged.

"You're a terrible loser," he teased, his voice a low rumble that sent shivers down my spine.

"And you're an insufferable winner," I shot back, though the bite I intended fell flat, my breath catching in my throat.

His lips curved into a grin, the kind that made my knees weak and my mind race. "Want me to make it up to you?" he murmured, his voice impossibly soft yet filled with promise.

Before I could reply, his hand came up to brush my cheek. The simple touch was enough to send my pulse skyrocketing. He traced the line of my jaw with his thumb, his touch unhurried, as though he was memorizing the shape of me. I didn't breathe. I couldn't.

"Malik..." His name was barely a whisper, a plea, but I wasn't even sure what I was asking for.

He leaned closer, his body towering over mine but not pressing, his presence commanding every ounce of my attention. His lips hovered just above mine, teasing, the faintest brush of his breath ghosting across my skin. I felt his hands slide to my waist, his fingers splaying against my dress, and I was sure he could feel me shaking beneath his touch.

"Tell me to stop," he said, his voice rough, his lips so close they brushed mine as he spoke.

I swallowed hard, my resolve crumbling as the tension between us snapped like a taut wire. "Don't you dare."

His lips crashed against mine, the sudden intensity stealing the breath from my lungs. It wasn't gentle. It wasn't tentative. It was a kiss that demanded everything and left no room for second thoughts. His mouth moved against mine with a hunger that matched my own, his teeth grazing my bottom lip as his hand slid up my back, pulling me impossibly closer.

The world tilted, narrowed. All I could feel was him—the heat of his body, the strength of his hands, the way his lips tasted of tequila. My fingers tangled in his hair, tugging him closer as my back pressed harder against the wall. His stubble scraped against my skin in the most delicious way, sending sparks skittering down my spine.

He deepened the kiss, his tongue brushing against mine in a making me gasp. His other hand trailed down my side, his thumb tracing the curve of my hip before gripping it firmly. The pressure made me gasp against his mouth, and he took full advantage, his kiss growing bolder, more demanding.

I was unraveling, melting, every nerve in my body singing with the feel of him. The noises of the party faded to nothing, the entire universe shrinking down to the way Malik's lips fit against mine, the way his hands anchored me while simultaneously setting me adrift.

When he finally pulled back, it was only because we were both gasping for air. His forehead rested against mine, his breath warm against my skin, his hands still cradling my waist like he was afraid I might disappear. My eyes fluttered open to find him staring at me, his gaze dark and molten, his chest heaving.

"This isn't over," he murmured, his voice rough and full of promise.

I let out a shaky breath, my fingers still clutching his shirt. "I didn't think it was."

A slow smile spread across his lips. He dipped his head, brushing one last, lingering kiss against my swollen mouth before pulling away just enough to look at me fully. His thumb brushed over my cheek again, his eyes slowly drinking me in like he was memorizing every detail.

The sound of laughter from the party drifted back into focus, grounding me, but my body still hummed with electricity. Malik smirked, his hand trailing down to capture mine again. He laced our fingers together, the simple gesture intimate.

"Come on," he said, his voice still low, a teasing edge to it.

I was still trying to catch my breath as he led us back inside. He knew exactly what he was doing to me, and Jade's raised eyebrow and knowing grin only added to my flustered state.

"I'll be right back," he said, pulling his hand free from my grip. I watched him heading toward the DJ, my fingers already missing his warmth.

"Let me guess," Jade said, sidling up beside me. "You've got filthy plans for tonight."

I shook my head, unable to keep the smile from my lips. "Tomorrow."

"Lucky bitch," she said with a wink, raising her glass.

The rest of the party unfolded around us, but all I could think about was the way Malik's lips felt against mine and the promise of what tomorrow would bring.

I felt alive—not because of the crowd, not because of the party, but because of the man whose hand I never wanted to let go of.

Chapter 12

The sunlight streamed through the curtains of my bedroom, warm and golden, coaxing me awake. I stretched slowly, my body feeling lighter than it had in weeks. The events of last night drifted back to me in vivid, electric flashes—Fiona's meltdown, the party in full swing, the teasing banter, and... Malik.

I let out a slow breath, my hand brushing against my lips, which still tingled like they'd been branded. The memory of his kisses burned through me, searing and tender, stealing every rational thought from my mind. It hadn't been just a kiss—it was a declaration. A claiming. The way his hands had gripped me like I was the only thing tethering him to this plane of existence made my heart race all over again.

And then, when he'd walked me to my door after the party...

My skin flushed just thinking about it. The soft hum of the city had wrapped around us, and I'd barely managed a whispered goodnight before he'd silenced me with his lips. It had been slower and more reverent. His hand cupped the back of my neck, his thumb tracing my skin as if memorizing every curve of me. Each stroke of his tongue and graze of his lips had me feeling like he was savoring me.

I could still feel the warmth of his palm there, could still taste something indescribably Malik lingering on my tongue. He'd pulled away, his forehead resting against mine, his breath warm and steady, grounding me when I'd felt like I might float away.

"Sleep well, Cass," he'd murmured, his voice low and full of unspoken promises.

And then he'd left, just like that, leaving me leaning against my door, my legs boneless, my heart beating so hard I was surprised I hadn't shattered my ribs.

But now.

Now that I'd had time to sleep. I felt... good. Hopeful.

For the first time in years, I wasn't waiting for the other shoe to drop.

A knock at the door pulled me out of my thoughts. I padded over, tying my robe around me, I opened it to find Malik standing there, holding two to-go cups of coffee and a giant breakfast burrito, looking devastatingly handsome in a light gray shirt and jeans.

"Good morning, sleepyhead," he said, his grin doing things to my body that a cup of coffee could never do.

"You're awfully chipper," I teased, taking the coffee gratefully. "What's the occasion?"

He leaned casually against the door frame, his eyes glinting with mischief. "We've got plans today. Big ones."

I raised an eyebrow, sipping the steaming coffee. "Oh? Should I be worried?"

His grin widened. "Come on, get dressed. The day's a-wasting."

"You're not even going to tell me what we're doing?" I asked, hand on my hip as I sipped the perfect latte.

"Where's the fun in that? Now, the key to your distraction-free adventure is one cell phone and eating half of this burrito."

I wanted to push, but something about the way he said it made my heart do a little flip. It had been so long since anyone had gone out of their way for me—not because they had to, but because they wanted to.

He made it seem effortless, like it wasn't even a question.

Everything about this new foundation we were building together both terrified and thrilled me. But I wasn't going to let the fear stop me. I'd had a taste, and that was enough for me to want more. I grabbed my phone from my pajama pocket and handed it to him.

"Come in, give me fifteen minutes," I said, turning back into my apartment. "And the burrito better have bacon in it."

"Your half does, I would never disrespect you like that," he said as he shut the door.

The next four hours passed in a haze of relaxation and luxury. The first stop was a spa. It was a decadent haven of tranquility. Soft piano music played in the background, and the air was scented with eucalyptus and lavender.

We started with a couples' massage in a room bathed in pink and yellow light, the tension in my shoulders melting under some very skilled hands. I caught Malik stealing glances at me through the soft veil of steam rising from the aromatherapy diffuser, his eyes lingering on me just long enough to make my cheeks warm.

The massage therapist's hands worked some straight-up witchcraft on the knots in my shoulders and back. It was like the weight of the last few years melted right out of my body as I closed my eyes and let it all go. The calm peace I was feeling was so different, I almost felt like a whole new person.

Afterward, we lounged in a private whirlpool surrounded by flickering candles. The water was milky white. He'd turned to give me a minute when I got in, and I did the same for him, but that didn't stop me from appreciating the sight of water clinging to his tattoos and glistening in the candlelight.

He leaned back, his arm resting casually along the edge, while I floated beside him, letting the warm water ease every knot and worry out of my body.

"I could get used to this," I murmured, my head tilted back as I closed my eyes.

"Good," he said, his voice low and teasing. "That's the point." He shifted slightly, splashing water onto my arm in the process. I opened one eye, shooting him a look.

"You're ruining the vibe," I said.

He chuckled, a soft, deep sound that wrapped around me and splashed me again—this time on purpose.

"Malik," I warned with a smile.

"What?" he asked, faux innocence dripping from his tone.

"You just want me to slip up so you can look at my goodies," I drawled, shaking my head.

"So?" he tilted his head and gave me one of those amused looks that made my cheeks heat.

"Stay on your side, you fiend," I said.

He kissed his teeth. "Fine. I will. This time."

Something about this man really had just snuck up on me. Reaching over, I found his hand with mine and gave it a squeeze.

"Thank you," I said softly, looking over at him.

He glanced at me, his smile soft and genuine. "For what?"

"For this. For everything," I said, gesturing vaguely. "You didn't have to—"

"I wanted to," he interrupted, his voice firm but kind. "You deserve it."

Breaking eye contact, I looked toward the flickering candles, trying to process the way he made me feel—cherished, seen, and safe, all at once.

When was the last time I let myself just be? I wondered, closing my eyes and letting the warm water lull me into a rare moment of peace. My mind drifted to Malik's smile, to the way he'd brushed a thumb over my cheek earlier, his touch as natural as breathing. He made it look so easy, like taking care of me was second nature.

And for the first time in years, I didn't feel the urge to push it away.

The second stop was an art studio. It was all jewel tones and ambiance as we went inside and headed straight to the back. Malik smiled at someone and waved, but he clearly knew his way around. The room was tiny. Soft, light spilled from hanging Edison bulbs, the faint scent of earth and clay mingling with lavender.

It should've been soothing. It should've been easy to focus. But how was I supposed to relax when he was looking at me like that and bringing back memories? Making me wonder what else he could do with those strong thighs and talented hands.

His gaze burned into me as he set down a tray of tools, his grin just a little too cocky. I tightened my fist, determined to act like I wasn't affected. But I was. The memory of his fingers digging into my waist, his lips trailing over mine, it was still seared into my skin, living rent-free in my head.

"This is... unexpected," I said, gesturing to the pottery wheel.

"I come here sometimes to clear my head. Consider this step two on your ladder to bliss."

Malik leaned against the table, his arms crossing over his chest. The soft fabric of his shirt stretched across his shoulders, and for a second, I forgot how to breathe.

"You mean brilliant," he corrected. His voice dipped into that low, teasing tone that made my stomach tighten. "Come on, Cass. You can't tell me you're not intrigued."

Before I could reply, he grabbed an apron from the rack and walked toward me, his eyes locking on mine. "Turn around."

The command was soft but firm. My heart stuttered, but I did as he asked, feeling the weight of his eyes following my body as I turned my back to him.

I heard the rustle of fabric, then felt it—his hands brushing against my shoulders as he slipped the apron over my head. His touch was maddeningly light, the barest graze of his fingers against my neck making me shiver. He reached around my waist to tie the strings, and I was acutely aware of his knuckles brushing against my skin, the heat of his body so close I could feel it through the thin shirt.

"Perfect," he murmured, his breath skimming over my ear.

I swallowed hard, trying to ignore the fire spreading through me. "You do this for all your pottery students?" I asked, my voice too breathy for my liking.

"Just the special ones," he said, stepping back, but not far enough for me to fully catch my breath.

I turned to face him, arching an eyebrow. "So, what's the plan, Swayze?"

"Let's see what you've got," he said with a wink, motioning for me to move toward the wheel.

I moved forward, determined to keep my focus. The clay was cold and pliable beneath my fingers. I looked down and found the pedal that turned the wheel and pressed down on it, watching the clay slowly spin with a steady hum.

He glanced at me, his mocking grin mischievous. "Need help?"

"No," I lied, determined not to give him the satisfaction.

Taking a breath, I pushed at the clay, watching as it barely moved. I squished it, annoyed that it wasn't moving the way I wanted.

He chuckled, low and deep. "Not bad. For a first-timer."

I shot him a look. "Oh, you're hilarious."

"Here," he said, moving forward. "Let me help."

"Malik, I can—"

But he was already there, his hands closing over mine before I could stop him. He used our hands to scoop water from a bowl to my right. I sucked in a breath as his fingers pressed against mine, firm but gentle, guiding us back to the center of the clay. His thumbs brushed the inside of my wrists, sending jolts of heat straight through me.

"Relax," he murmured, his lips dangerously close to my ear. "You're too tense."

My hands slipped against the spinning clay, my focus shot to hell the moment Malik leaned in closer. His breath brushed my temple, warm and distracting. It was enough to make my pulse flutter, my movements falter.

"I wonder why," I muttered, my voice unsteady.

His chuckle was a low rumble vibrating through my back as he leaned closer. "You have to feel the clay. Let it guide you. Don't fight it. That's it. Keep it spinning."

The wheel spun, the clay beginning to take shape beneath our hands, but I couldn't focus. Not with Malik standing so close, his breath warm against my neck, his fingers moving over mine with maddening precision. Every touch was deliberate, every brush of his skin against mine sending a ripple of awareness through me.

"See?" he said, his voice rougher now. "It's not so hard."

"Sure," I said low.

He leaned in closer, bringing himself flush against me. "You're doing great, Cass," he murmured, his tone softer now, almost intimate. "But I think you can do better."

The words hung between us, heavy and charged. His hands shifted slightly, his fingers trailing over mine as he adjusted the pressure. The clay curved under our combined touch, smooth and even, but all I could feel was him—the heat of his body, the strength in his grip, the way his voice wrapped around me like a cocoon.

Our hands were creating a misshapen pot, but I was absolutely no longer interested in the clay transforming before my eyes.

I was interested in the way he slowly coached my body with his. I turned my head slightly, catching his gaze. His eyes were dark, molten, filled with an intensity that made my pulse race.

"Malik..." My voice wavered, a warning and a plea all at once.

His lips curved into a slow, devastating smile. "Yeah?"

The wheel slowed to a stop, and the noise of the studio seeped back in, grounding me just enough to realize how breathless I was. My hands were still in his, the clay now forgotten as we stared at each other, the air between us charged and heavy with unspoken promises.

Malik's eyes flicked from the clay-streaked mess of our hands to my face, his expression softer now, less teasing. His thumb moved in lazy circles over my knuckles, and my heart thudded so hard I was sure he could hear it.

"You're dangerous," I murmured, trying to sound unaffected, though my voice betrayed me with its unsteady quiver.

"Me?" He tilted his head, a slow grin spreading across his face. "You're the one who just made this a contact sport."

I couldn't help the laugh that bubbled out of me, breaking the tension for a moment—but only a moment.

His gaze stayed fixed on me, warm and steady, a look that made the rest of the world fall away.

I didn't think—I just acted. Leaning forward, I kissed him slowly, savoring the way his lips parted against mine. The kiss wasn't rushed or frantic; it was measured, as though we were both finally giving in to something we'd been holding back for far too long.

His hands found my waist, pulling me closer until there was nothing between us but the sound of our breathing and the quiet hum of the studio.

When I finally pulled back, my lips tingling and my heart racing, he was watching me like I'd just done something miraculous.

"What?" I asked, suddenly self-conscious under the weight of his gaze.

"Nothing," he replied, his smile crooked and impossibly endearing. "I'm just... happy."

I leaned up and kissed his neck. "Let's get out of here," I murmured, my lips barely brushing his ear as I spoke.

"Thank Christ," he said with a low chuckle, his hand trailing up my arm.

My heart was pounding, and my mind was a mess of swirling thoughts. The most prominent: I was about to fuck Malik's brains out.

Chapter 13

I felt like I was walking on a wire—each step taut, each moment a precarious balance between giving in and holding on. And every time I looked over at him, with that slow, knowing smile on his lips, I wondered why I was bothering trying to balance at all.

It was scary, how easily he fit into my life. How effortlessly he slipped past my defenses. And scarier still was how much I wanted him there

"Still thinking about your masterpiece?" Malik asked, his voice warm and teasing as he nudged my shoulder.

I'd run to the bathroom to clean my hands and the ocean that my panties had become, and now we were walking towards where he'd parked.

I laughed, the sound light but shaky. "I think it's safe to say no museums will be calling me anytime soon."

"Oh, I don't know about that," he said, his eyes dipping to my lips before flicking back up to meet mine. "I think it deserves a special spot on display. Right in my living room."

"Your living room?" I echoed, my cheeks heating.

His grin widened, and he took a step closer, his hand brushing mine. "Of course. A personal gallery of Cass James originals. I'll charge admission."

I rolled my eyes, though the flutter in my chest betrayed me. "You're ridiculous."

"Maybe," he said softly, his voice dropping just enough to make my stomach flip. "But I'd still display it. It's not about the pot," he said, his voice soft, "It's about what you let yourself feel."

I froze, his words hitting deeper than I expected. He stepped closer. "Cass, you don't have to have all the answers all the time. You just have to let yourself be open."

The air between us thickened, the easy humor morphing into something heavier, something charged. The rumble of passing cars became a distant murmur. It felt like the world was giving us permission to pause, to let the space between us fill with unspoken possibilities.

"My place?" he asked.

The invitation was casual on the surface, but his tone held something more—a quiet challenge, a promise.

I hesitated for only a fraction of a second before nodding. "Sure."

"Good," he said, his voice like a caress. He placed his hand on the small of my back, guiding me toward his car.

As he opened the passenger door for me, his fingers lingered on my skin, sending shivers down my spine. His gaze caught mine, and for a moment, I thought he might kiss me again, right there on the curb.

But he didn't.

Instead, he smiled—a slow, devastating curve of his lips that had me catching my breath—and closed the door once I slid inside.

The drive to his house was full of a comfortable and pleasant silence that didn't need to be filled. Malik's hand rested on the gear shift, but every so often, his fingers would brush against mine, a casual touch that sent sparks dancing across my skin.

"I'm glad you didn't fight me on today," he said suddenly, his voice breaking the quiet.

"Why would I fight you?" I asked, my lips curving into a smile.

He glanced at me, his expression warm. "Because you're you. And you don't like letting people in."

The truth of his words hit me harder than I expected, but instead of denying it, I gave him a small smile, "Maybe you're the exception."

His eyes lit up as he smiled at me. "I like being the exception."

I'd spent years building walls around my heart, learning how to stay safe behind them. But here I was, sitting in Malik's car, his hand brushing against mine like it was the most natural thing in the world. Every touch chipped away at my defenses, leaving me exposed in ways that brought my body out of hibernation.

But I didn't stop him. I didn't want to.

When we pulled into his driveway, the sun was starting to sink. The air was thick with anticipation as he came around to open my door. His hand grabbed mine as I stepped out, his grip steady and reassuring.

He touched my cheek as he held me still. "Is this okay?" he murmured, his voice impossibly soft.

I nodded, my lips brushing against his palm as I met his gaze and whispered, "Yes."

Inside, the atmosphere shifted. The quiet intimacy of his space wrapped around us, the faint scent of cedar and something warm and familiar filling the air. With him, the world outside seemed to fade. There was only the sound of my breath, ragged and uneven, and the way his gaze never left mine.

"You want water? Wine?" Malik asked, his voice low and smooth as he stepped into the kitchen. I opened my mouth to answer, but the words caught in my throat when he turned, leaning casually against the counter, his eyes smoldering. The offer felt like a formality, like we both knew the only thing I wanted wasn't in a glass.

I shook my head slowly as I walked over to him.

"You know, you have this way of..." I trailed off, unsure how to finish the sentence without saying too much.

His brow lifted in question, but instead of pressing me, he reached over and brushed a streak of dry clay off my cheek with his thumb. The touch was so light, so intentional, it sent a ripple of heat through me.

"I have a way of what?" he asked, his voice dipping into that lower register that always turned my knees to jelly.

"Of... this." I gestured vaguely between us, feeling like an idiot but unable to articulate what I meant. "Of making everything else feel... insignificant."

His grin faded into something softer, something real. "Good," he said, his voice quiet but firm. "Because when I'm with you, Cass, nothing else matters."

I swallowed hard, my pulse skittering wildly. There was no teasing now, no playful banter. Just Malik, raw and open, laying his cards on the table. And I wanted to do the same.

I didn't reply. I couldn't. I took a steadying breath.

His gaze darkened and he held out his hand. I stepped into his arms, leaning up to look into his eyes as his hand found my cheek. "Cass..."

My heart pounded as I whispered, "Yeah?"

He didn't answer—not with words, anyway. Instead, he kissed me, it was a promise of things I wasn't sure I was ready for, I knew I wouldn't be able to bring myself to resist. Not anymore.

I didn't think. I didn't hesitate. I just pulled him toward his bedroom, my pulse thundering in my ears.

Chapter 14

His bedroom was just as warm and comfortable as the rest of his apartment. Hitting the lights, I watched as he emptied his pockets out on the dresser. The bedside lamps cast shadows across the room as Malik stepped back, his chest rising and falling in measured breaths.

"We need to eat," he said, his voice low, rough, teasing, like he was battling every instinct to let the moment stretch just a little longer. He brought his hands to my waist, and I smiled at him.

"Food?" I murmured, breathless and entirely unconvincing.

The grin he shot me was devastating, full of mischief and heat. "Food first," his voice dipped, softer, "then I'll have my dessert."

I swallowed hard, my entire body a live wire under his touch. "Food can wait."

He pulled back, his thumb brushing over my cheek, his gaze so intense it felt like a touch. "You'll need the energy," he murmured.

My breath caught in my throat, and the little devious grin tugging at the corner of his lips told me he knew exactly what he was doing to me. He pressed a chaste kiss to my forehead—so infuriatingly sweet—before stepping back entirely.

"Malik," I said, half a protest, half a plea.

"Patience," he teased as he reached for his phone. His fingers moved over the screen as he ordered us something to eat.

I watched him, my pulse hammering in my throat as he nodded to his phone before setting it back down. He didn't even have the decency to look rushed.

"What did you order?" I asked, trying desperately to regain some shred of the sanity that had been kissed out of me.

"Other than you?" he asked, his gaze sweeping over me.

I huffed, shaking my head. "You're ridiculous."

"Hmm," he said, his voice softer now as he closed the distance between us again. His hands found my hips, pulling me against him as his lips brushed my temple, my cheek, the corner of my mouth.

My hands slid up his chest, fisting lightly in the fabric of his shirt. "How long do we have?"

"Forty-five minutes," he murmured, his lips tracing a slow path down my jaw to my neck.

"That's too long," I whispered, tilting my head to give him more access, my breath catching as his lips grazed my ear.

"Then I guess I'll have to keep you occupied," he said, his voice low and rough as his hands slid lower, his thumbs brushing the curve of my hips.

"Occupied, huh?" My words were barely audible, my heart thundering as his lips moved lower, pressing open-mouthed kisses to my collarbone.

"Mm-hmm," he hummed, sinking to his knees before me.

His hands trailed down my thighs, his fingers curling around my calves as his molten gaze locked onto mine.

The air in the room shifted, growing heavier, hotter, as Malik's hands found the skin beneath my jeans, his touch light and hypnotic.

"Let me take care of you, Cass," he murmured, his voice like velvet, coaxing, commanding.

The only response I could manage was a shaky nod, my knees trembling as his hands gripped the backs of my thighs, his touch firm and anchoring, grounding me even as I felt like I was coming undone.

He pressed his mouth to my stomach, and I shivered. My hand came to the back of his head as his tongue peeked out, tracing and sucking at my skin as his fingers touched my zipper, and he pulled it down, his lips tracing a line from my belly down to my thigh.

Every graze of skin against mine made me shiver as pleasure and anticipation warred within me. When he finished his path down to my leg, I stepped out of my pants and shoes. He traced a similar path back up my body, licking and sucking at my skin as he made his way back up to my belly.

Finding his feet, his lips crashed against mine in a kiss that stole the very air from my lungs. The kiss was desperate, hungry, and I answered it with a ferocity that matched his own. His hands slid down my back, pulling me flush against him, and I moaned, feeling his length pushing against his jeans. I found him with my hands, dragging my fingers up as he pushed me back towards the bed. Malik's hands gripped my hips as the backs of my knees hit the edge of the mattress. His tongue swept into my mouth, claiming every inch, leaving me breathless and lightheaded.

As I fell back onto the bed, he followed, his weight pressing me into the mattress. The heat of him was intoxicating, his body soft and strong above me. His hand slipped under my shirt, the grip of his fingers doing things to my insides.

I arched into his touch, my own hands tugging at the hem of his shirt. "Off," I whispered, my voice a mix of urgency and need.

He pulled back just enough to yank the fabric over his head, the sight of his bare chest stealing whatever breath I had left. The tattoos that marked his skin seemed to ripple with the movement, and I couldn't help but reach out, tracing the ink with my fingers.

"Yours too," he said, his voice sending fire straight through my veins.

My shirt was gone in seconds, and his lips were back on my skin, scorching a blazing trail from my collarbone to the swell of my breasts.

I tangled my fingers in his hair as his tongue teased me. His mouth grazed my breast through my bra, just enough to make my body arch beneath him.

He growled low in his throat, the sound vibrating against my skin as he trailed kisses lower, his hands sliding down to grip my thighs. He looked up at me, his eyes filled with desire as pleasure warmed my skin. The way his gaze held mine, molten and fervent, made me feel like I was the only thing in the world he wanted.

It was thrilling. Overwhelming. Addictive.

His lips curved into a wicked smile before he pressed a kiss to my inner thigh, his hands slowly parting my legs. The anticipation was almost unbearable, every nerve in my body was alight as I waited for his next move.

And when his mouth finally found me, his tongue was everything he was—warm and sweet. I groaned. He wasn't tentative, he was relentless. Every stroke of his tongue, every gentle scrape of his teeth, unraveled me piece by piece. My fingers grabbed the back of the pillow as he pulled waves of pleasure from my body. His grip on my thighs was firm, keeping me anchored even as I jerked against his mouth.

He hummed against me, the vibrations sending a jolt of heat straight through me. My hips bucked, seeking more, and he didn't hold back. His tongue moved with precision, circling and finding the perfect angle on my clit that made me moan his name over and over.

Tension coiled tighter and tighter as I bucked in an easy cadence against his face. His hands slid up, one splaying across my stomach to keep me steady, the other teasing the sensitive skin of my inner thigh. He looked up at me, his gaze intense.

His questing hand grabbed mine and placed it on the back of his head as he pulled my clit into his mouth and sucked. The pressure was delicious and intense and all I needed to orgasm. My back arched as my body detonated.

I cried out, shuddering as the pleasure ripped through me, stealing the air from my lungs. He didn't stop, his sucking became more meticulous as he slowly drew out every last tremor. He held me to him, drawing out each gasping shudder with delicious ease.

When I finally stilled, my chest heaving and my limbs trembling, he kissed his way back up my body, his lips soft and reverent against my flushed skin.

I wasn't sure how I was still breathing, let alone conscious. He wasn't just touching me, he was consuming me, piece by piece, like I was something precious he wanted to savor. He hovered over me, his gaze tender yet filled with heat as he wiped sweat from my damp forehead.

I pulled him down for a kiss, tasting myself on his lips. The way he deepened the kiss, made my heart race all over again.

I wrapped my legs around his waist, feeling the hard press of him against my thigh. My hands slid down his back, basking in the heat of his skin. "Your turn," I said, my voice a husky promise.

Malik's lips brushed mine as he whispered, "Not yet."

He moved back down my body, fixing his mouth right back to me, making me cry out and hold him to me as he placed two fingers deep inside me. Clenching down, I moaned, glad that he wasn't done with me.

I shivered in delight as he stoked my pleasure in a way that proved he knew exactly what I needed and was willing to give me all of it.

I just had to let him.

Chapter 15

Dinner was a delicious mess of takeout boxes spread across Malik's couch, their tempting aromas blending with the subtle scent of cedar that lingered in the air.

I sat cross-legged, my naked ass wrapped in a throw blanket he'd draped over my shoulders, the soft fabric a stark contrast to the fire that still simmered in my veins. Across from me, he leaned back, shirtless, his broad shoulders relaxed, his dark eyes glinting with a mix of satisfaction and mischief.

I speared a piece of orange chicken with my fork, pausing to admire the way the light of the bedside lamp cast shadows over his chest, highlighting the tattoos etched into his skin.

"I think this might be the most delicious meal I've ever had. Post-massage, post... snack."

"Food tastes better when you've earned it," he teased, his voice dripping with suggestion. His coy smile was devastatingly handsome as he popped a piece of broccoli into his mouth.

I rolled my eyes, though my smile gave me away. "Does that make me the appetizer and dessert?"

He leaned forward, his gaze taking a slow path from my eyes to my lips and back. "Yes. And I'm pacing myself."

"Pacing yourself?" I arched a brow, fighting to keep my voice steady even as heat crept up my neck.

His smile widened as he leaned back, his long legs stretched out in front of him. "I've got plans for you, Cass, and I'm not rushing through them."

A laugh bubbled out of me, genuine and unrestrained, and it filled the room in a way that felt new and right. "You're ridiculous."

"And you love it," he said, his tone softening as he held my gaze.

I opened my mouth to respond with something equally teasing, but the words stuck in my throat. Because he was right. And for once, I didn't want to deflect.

"Maybe I do," I said quietly, the admission hanging between us.

His smirk faded, replaced by something deeper, something that made my chest tighten. He leaned over, stealing a kiss like it was the most natural thing in the world.

"Well," he said, his voice lower, quieter, "I'm definitely keeping you."

After dinner, the energy shifted. Playful banter gave way to soft touches, stolen glances, and an unspoken current of anticipation that hummed between us like electricity.

I was laughing at something Malik had said, my head tilted back against the cushions, when I felt his hand on mine, his thumb brushing over my knuckles.

"Cass," he murmured, his voice low and rough, filled with something that made my laughter fade and my pulse quicken.

I turned to face him, my breath catching as his gaze dropped to my lips. "Hmm?"

He didn't answer—not with words. Instead, he leaned in, his lips brushing the corner of my mouth in a way that made my stomach flip.

His hand slid to my hip, tugging me gently onto his lap, and I went willingly, leaving the blanket behind. My arms wrapping around his neck as our mouths met in a kiss that was hot, building in intensity with every passing second.

"Didn't you just say something about pacing yourself?" I whispered against his lips, my voice breathless as his hands skimmed up my waist, grabbing on to my love handles.

"I changed my mind," he murmured, his lips tracing a line along my jaw to my neck.

I sighed into his kisses, feeling my body still slick and ready for him. His fingers touched the sides of my thighs, grabbing at them and placing my heat right on top of him. Rolling my hips, I heard him hiss against my skin.

My fingers went to his pants, unbuckling them. When I had them undone, I dipped my fingers between my folds before leaning back and feeding them to him. His tongue swirled and sucked as I leaned up so he could shimmy out of his jeans.

I sat back, feeling the weight of him, hot against my soaking core, as I slowly rocked my hips back and forth along his length. My tongue explored the skin of his neck as I sucked and bit at him, tracing a line up to his ear.

"I need to take it slow," I whispered.

His fingers dug into the fabric of the couch, and I felt a thrill of triumph racing through me. He was at my mercy.

I sucked his skin into my mouth and his hand found my hips, helping me set the pace against my clit.

My fingers came to his length, pulling up and down, on him. He moaned, and I felt him harden in my grip.

Lining him up, I slowly angled my body and pulled him inside me. I let out a breath, feeling the familiar stretch and burn. Pausing, I held his shoulders, closing my eyes and trying to relax.

"Hey," he said.

I looked down at him. His forehead shimmered with sweat as I took a gasping breath.

"Look at me," he whispered.

"It's been a while," I said, my eyes misting.

"Take it slow. I'm here for a long time and a good time," he answered, his hands running up and down on my skin.

I cackled before I brought my lips to his, hoping he understood how appreciative I was of him being the person I was doing this with. Our tongues tangled and I took in more of his length. We moaned together, as I slowly rocked up and down taking more and more of him.

He let out a groan when I was fully seated on him, his dick touching all the parts of me that I knew he would. His fingers rubbed my clit, and I smacked at the couch as the pain gave way to pleasure.

"Fuck," I groaned out, arching.

His mouth covered my neck, sucking at my skin as I started to bounce on his length. His other hand grabbed my waist, helping me move up and down on him. My head lolled back as his slick fingers discovered the perfect pressure to put on my clit as he moved his thumb over me.

Pleasure flooded through me as I angled my hips and rocked into the perfect angle that had me panting. I grabbed his shoulders, wanting more. I began bouncing on him, feeling him stroking along my walls and making me clench tight around him.

He kept his pressure on my clit as I started talking to him, saying all the things I'd been unable to say before.

"The way you make me feel."

"That's it right there."

"Why are you so good to me?"

"You are perfect."

My hips found a better pace as my thighs opened, inviting him in. The sounds of me squelching down on him had me ready to bust, and I fought it. I needed more, I leaned forward, finding my feet and bouncing up and down on him.

His fingers left my clit so he could move down and let me find a deeper angle that had me calling out his name. I moaned as his hands clenched around my waist and guided my movement.

"Yes," I moaned, seeing concern and lust warring on his face. "More, please. More."

My hips hit a swinging thrust that had me so close to orgasm that my vision was getting blurry. I grabbed his shoulders, as he helped my hips find the right angle and rhythm.

When the orgasm hit, I stilled as wave after wave rolled through me, making my legs shake and my insides clench. My hand came down on his shoulder as I tried to ride out each wave. That's when his hips kept a slow push underneath me, drawing out my pleasure and making me cry out.

"Fuck." I screamed, my mouth finding his shoulder as my orgasm kept going with his every stroke.

His hand twirled on my clit, and I wheezed, feeling my whole body convulse above him.

"Wait," I breathed. "It's too good."

"Good," he hissed, keeping his hips moving and building on all the pleasure, making me breathe hard as his dick moved methodically in and out of me, sliding right against my sensitive flesh.

I could feel my legs shaking, but that didn't stop him. He pushed me up and down until I threw my head back and another orgasm tore through me. Grabbing his hands, I felt his mouth trailing a line to my bra, pulling my breast free to suck my nipple, twirling and biting down on the sensitive bud.

My hand came to the back of his head as pleasure continued to roll through me as I came down. I stopped moving my hips against him and just soaked in the feeling of being full of him. Tears were falling from my eyes as I caught my breath and found my equilibrium.

His mouth eased off my nipple, moving up my chest, licking and nipping at my skin as he went. Wrenching my neck to the side, he bit down, pulling hard at my skin.

"You get sixty more seconds before I make you forget your name," he moaned in my ear.

I laughed, breathless. "Oh really?"

He brought his fingers back to my clit, rolling it beneath his fingers as he sucked my neck.

And just like that, passion robbed my lungs of breath and everything fell away but us.

Chapter 16

When my legs finally gave out, we made it back to the bedroom. I couldn't remember how. All I knew was that I was growing addicted to the warmth of Malik's hands on my skin, the steady cadence of his breath against my ear, and the way his body felt on top of mine.

This time, he was in control. And I was more than okay with the way his hands revered every curve of my body with absolutely no urgency. Everything about his touch was careful. He was treating me like a fragile glass sculpture, and it made this feel like something more.

It cracked me open, leaving me feeling raw and open beneath him. But I trusted him. I knew I could be all of the versions of myself with him because he saw everything that I'd tried to hide and cared for me because of that, not in spite of it.

His mouth moved across me, like he was memorizing me. Every time I sighed or moaned, I felt him pause, like he was taking notes and keeping track. His touch was almost worshipful as he discovered new spots and ways to drive me wild.

And when he finally filled me again, I was practically begging for it. His breath huffed past my ear as he gave me his weight, his hands holding my thighs as he thrusted. He stilled for a moment, his body vibrating.

I tried to stay still, but I clenched down on him and he whimpered before groaning. The fingers gripping my thighs tightened as he grunted, moving in and out slowly. I absolutely needed him to move. Really move.

"Malik," I moaned.

"Yeah, baby?" he whispered, looking at me.

"Stop. Fucking. Teasing. Me."

He laughed hard before pulling his hips all the way back and slamming back into me. Then it was my turn to whimper. Each thrust was powerful, rocking me up the bed and moving me closer to the headboard.

He used all of his length to tease every inch of me, and I was ready to climb into his skin as he continued his deep, rocking cadence. His tongue came out to wet his lips, and I started to move my hips to meet each thrust. I could play that game too.

He moaned again, and I could tell he was cracking. When he filled me again, I ran my nails along his ass and clenched tight around him.

A gasping growl left his mouth, and he sat up, pulling my hips back and putting my legs on his shoulders. His hips dove deep, digging all the way into my insides and I cried out, feeling him everywhere.

But he was just getting started.

It was almost like he was waiting for me to give him the cue because the way his thrusts had me hurtling into and past one orgasm and then the next, I was sure I was going to have to tap out. But I couldn't. I wanted every single touch, every pulse, every thrust, and I wasn't going to stop until both of us were spent.

With the way he was fucking me, I just hoped I didn't fall apart into a million pieces by the time he came. His dick hit a new angle that had me hollering as I clenched down on him, my fingers clutching at the sheets as I saw stars.

He leaned down, his mouth finding mine as he pumped harder into me, drawing out the pulsing orgasm that had me running for the headboard. He held me down grunting as he kept fucking me.

I was sure the things that left my mouth were pure nonsense. I was shaking as my eyes rolled back when the next orgasm hit. I couldn't breathe. The air left my lungs and my whole nervous system short-circuited. When my ears stopped ringing, Malik's jagged moans were music to my ears as he pulled out just in time to cum on me, thick streams coating my belly.

We were both breathing hard and covered in sweat. He collapsed beside me and stared up at the ceiling as I tried to lower my blood pressure with deep breaths. I was probably very close to stroking out. And I was okay with that.

Hell, that man had me so wrung out, he could've tattooed his name across my titties, and I'd have been okay with it. I had never in my entire life been fucked like that, and it was both thrilling and raw.

"You're incredible," he murmured, his voice rough with emotion, he leaned over his brown eyes searching mine.

I swallowed hard, my chest tightening at the intensity in his gaze.

"I mean it," he said, his thumb brushing over my cheek in a gesture so tender it made my breath hitch.

"You're everything, Malik. I don't know how I got so fucking lucky." Tears pricked at the corners of my eyes as I reached up, cupping his face in my hands before he pulled me into his arms.

Time stretched and blurred, the room filled with the quiet hum of our breathing. In his arms, I felt weightless, whole, and utterly cherished.

As the night stretched on, we talked about everything and nothing—about our favorite childhood memories, our biggest fears, and the little things that made us who we were. And somewhere between laughter and quiet confessions, I realized something I hadn't dared to hope for in years.

For the first time, I wasn't afraid of what came next.

Because whatever it was, I knew we'd face it together.

As Malik's breathing slowed, his chest rising and falling in a steady rhythm beneath my cheek, I smiled to myself, my fingers tracing the edge of the small moon and starts tattoo on his ribs that matched my own.

"Whatever happens next," I whispered, my voice steady, "we've got this."

Epilogue

A year later

Life had changed so much in the past year that it was hard for me to fathom it. But I'd finally gotten back to our—insert internal squee here because what!?—apartment. I was still getting used to sharing space with someone else, let alone a big old tattooed man that made me drip like a leaky faucet just by looking at me.

Shutting the door, I saw our misshapen clay pot on the coffee table. It was a reminder of how far we'd come and the way that we'd found one another through the muck and the chaos. My day-to-day was different, but I always came home to him.

Us.

As much as I'd been dreading it, the influencer work wasn't as bad as I thought it would be. I'd struck a good balance of which events I would attend or wouldn't and the money was great. Occasionally, they'd request that I bring Malik as my date to a restaurant and all we'd do is eat and take a photo, and we'd get a fat check.

Thankfully, my human version of a golden retriever didn't mind it. I actually think he secretly loved watching me get dressed up all fancy. I mean, if the way he completely demolished my insides afterward was any indication, he was practically salivating for more of those dates.

Speaking of breaking my back, I had to start doing yoga because I couldn't keep up with him. That first night was, in fact, not a fluke, and with the way, he was pile-driving me into the mattress, I had to start being more active to keep up.

I crept into the bathroom and took a quick shower, thinking I'd be quiet as hell and not wake him, but when I came out, he was sitting up, checking his phone.

"Hey," I said.

"Come here."

I tossed my clothes in the hamper and walked over, jumping into his arms. He squeezed me tight and kissed all over my face before throwing the covers over us both. The routine was so familiar, a part of me was happy he was a light sleeper.

I'd found someone who let me be soft. Maybe I didn't think I deserved this before, but with Malik... I knew I did.

"How's your ink?" he asked.

My gaze went to the small scrabble tile just above my left breast. It was healing quickly, the red *M* looked clean and bright.

"It's good, yours?" I asked, looking at the one he'd helped me tattoo on his chest.

"Perfect," he replied.

The fact that he'd let me tattoo him was actually insane.

I traced the *C* Scrabble tile as I thought about how much life had changed for us in the last year. His shop was booked out until the end of next year. And I was getting so burnt out on coffee shops that sometimes I'd make a thermos of instant and brought it with me to work.

My new normal was different, but that was okay because different was what I'd needed and asked the universe for when I was staring up at my cracked ceiling waiting for my life to start over again.

It wasn't at all what I'd expected, but it was the calm serenity I deserved.

His fingers brushed lightly over my arm, something he did when he was sketching in his brain.

"You're quiet," he said softly, his voice breaking the comfortable silence.

"Just thinking," I replied, my lips curving into a smile.

"About tomorrow?" he asked, pulling me closer.

I looked up at him, my fingers stilling against his skin. "Nah. Rosemary's team is so on top of it. I barely had anything to do."

Having Rosemary sponsor Love Me Not was incredible. She was handling everything, and I was actually able to step back and enjoy throwing it for once.

It had me feeling nostalgic for a time when it was me with a hope and a vibe. Even then, Malik was there.

He'd always been there.

"So?" he asked, dragging out the word as he ran his lips along my neck.

"I was thinking about you. Us, really. About how right this feels."

His hand slid up to cup my cheek, his thumb brushing over my skin in a way that made my chest ache. "Damn right. Let's get to sleep, we've got a long day tomorrow."

I pressed a kiss to his shoulder. "You're getting used to all this glitz and glamour."

He let out a laugh as I settled my head on to his shoulder. "It's those sexy little panties you wear under those dresses."

"Fiend," I said on a yawn.

Fingers pushed my hair from my face so he could look in my eyes. "Always," he whispered.

My stylist insisted on me wearing white this year. The dress hit me mid-thigh and the long sleeves covered my tatts. White was my least favorite color because I could never get through a day without spilling something on myself. But gin and tonics were clear, so maybe that would be my drink of choice tonight. She'd found stilettos that weren't terribly uncomfortable. My hair was curled and pinned over one shoulder. It was very demure.

A knock came at the door, and I opened it, surprised to see Jade and not my fine ass man.

"Babe. You look phenomenal. You ready?" she asked.

I gave her a look. "Are we waiting for Malik?" I asked, confused.

"Rosemary says that the livestream is already behind. We can't keep waiting." She gave me an apologetic look and I glanced around before taking a deep breath.

"He's not here? What's the point of driving that hearse on two wheels if he's not gonna be on time?"

It was fine. He'd make it up to me. At least six times. Maybe seven. I felt like setting a record.

"Okay, let's go."

We strode up the hallway and toward the event space. The security guard nodded at me and opened the door to a very quiet room. I turned to look at Jade, and she shoved me inside and closed the door.

A trail of flower petals and electric candles lined the path to the stage. Malik was standing there, clearly full of nervous energy. My mouth fell open as I looked between the spotlit path and him. Tears pooled in my eyes as I saw the trail that led to my happily ever after, and I couldn't move.

He gave me his sweet, wide smile. "Cass. Come here."

My heart was jackhammering in my chest.

"Are you sure? You can take it back. Pack up these lights and the rose petals might not keep, but you can dry them—"

"Cassia Calliope James. Come here." His eyebrows went up. He was dressed in all white, too, and I couldn't help but think he looked like he'd floated right off a cloud from heaven.

I willed my legs to move, walked across the pink petal-covered stage right to him. He held out his hand and I took it in mine.

Before I could stop myself, I kept talking, "You can—"

"Cassia. Stop talking and let me ask." He leaned forward and kissed my forehead before getting down on one knee.

"You are the most resilient woman I've ever met. You bring me joy and light, and I need that for the rest of my life. Love me always. Marry me?"

Tears welled in my eyes, but this time, I didn't try to fight them. I let them fall, allowing the moment to wash over me. He pulled a ring out of his pocket, and I didn't even look at it, I looked at him.

This man was everything I'd asked for and needed. He complemented me and challenged me and taught me to trust myself and learn to let go. I didn't know where I would be without him in my life. And I didn't want to find out.

His eyes were shining, and he looked worried, but he had that wide smile on his face that I loved to look at and that I wanted to keep seeing for forever. I dropped to my knees and grabbed his cheeks.

"Of course I will, Malik."

He pulled me into a hug, holding me tight to him as I heard cheering in the other room.

"What the—"

"The livestream," he whispered.

"Oh man, there's gonna be even more fanfiction now," I wailed.

He laughed, "It's kind of flattering that they give me such a big dick."

I shoved at him, trying to stand. "Why do you have to always bring that up?" I asked, rolling my eyes.

"If it wasn't big, you wouldn't want to marry me," he faux-whispered.

"Oh, for fuck's sake. We can all hear you. Put the ring on her finger so we can party." Jade yelled from the doorway.

He waggled his eyebrows at me as he slipped the gorgeous ring on my hand. The stone at the center was blue, and it was surrounded by glimmering pink, yellow, and red flowers.

It was perfect.

The doors opened, and the screaming crowd flooded in, holding up paper rings instead of paper hearts. I smiled and waved, leaning into him.

"I-I can't believe you want to be with me forever. You really see me," I said, my voice barely audible.

He looked over at me and wiped my tears away as I leaned into his touch.

"Cass. I'll always see you," he whispered, before standing and pulling me up with him.

Malik grabbed my waist and pulled me into his side as he shouted, "Welcome to *Love Me Always*!"

The crowd roared. A chant of, "Kiss! Kiss! Kiss!" rolled through the room.

He leaned towards me, whispering, "I'll never get tired of this," before his lips found mine.

Neither would I.

THE END

FROM AYLA'S DESK

Oh, hai!

Thank you so much for reading Malik and Cass's love story.

It's truly a blessing to be doing something I love every day knowing that it will reach who it's meant to.

As always, thank you so much for all of the positivity and life that you breath into me.

I still can't believe that this is really my life. That people find themselves in my words. And that I'm finding so much joy in something that used to scare the ever-loving shit out of me.

Your support is the reason why I continue to pick up my pen.

I appreciate and adore you all!

Until the next one, may your cup be ever full and your cum runneth over.

    Love,

    Tyla

ABOUT AYLA

Thank you for diving into Ayla Cox's world for a little while.

When Ayla's not on her knees in a fit of passion and lust, she's devouring any book she can get her hands on.

On the off chance that Ayla has time off, you may find her frolicking on a beach or hiding away in a lake cabin, recharging her batteries, both figuratively and literally.

If you love what you've read, give her a follow and leave a few encouraging words.

Sign up for her newsletter at:
https://www.aylacox.com/#newsletter

MORE FROM AYLA

Just a Taste Series
Tempted
Addicted
Insatiable

Standalones
12 Nights
Love Me Not

www.ingramcontent.com/pod-product-compliance
Lightning Source LLC
Chambersburg PA
CBHW022215190225
22256CB00023B/159